FALLEN KINGS: UNHOLY SECRETS

A Hillary Broome Crime Novel

ISBN: Print: 978-1-7324642-9-2

eBook: 978-1-7324642-8-5

Cover Design: Karen A. Phillips, www.phillipscovers.com

Formatting & Interior Design:

Tarra Thomas Indie Publishing Services.

Fallen Kings: Unholy Secrets

A Hillary Broome Crime Novel

June Gillam

For my mother Geraldine "Gerri" Capitolia Price Skalisky Robeson with gratitude for all I learned from her, a courageous crusader for women's rights in the Retail Clerk's Union.

Woman Found Dead in Trevi

By Angela Narratrice. BBC News• Updated: Thur - 06/015/2023

Italian police are hunting for the killer of a young woman discovered early Wednesday in the Trevi Fountain. A barista on his way to work described a slim figure dressed in black carrying something over his shoulder. "He dumped a bundle into the Trevi and ran off onto a side street."

Chamber of Deputies leader Elly Schlein expressed outrage and noted that Italy faces a "surge in femicides." Schlein, a leader in the LGBTQ rights movement, reported one of her aides missing after an explosion near the Coliseum during Rome's Pride Parade. "We hope these crimes are not connected." Identification of the victim is pending notification of family.

1
HILLARY

Hillary poured cream into her Intenso coffee to round out the bitterness. If only she could pour a mantle of protection around her teenaged daughter, Claire.

Claire's closet held plenty of rainbow-themed clothes, but she wanted something new for the Pride parade. Last night, she had searched through a stack of tee shirts at Walmart. She pressed a shirt against her chest to show Hillary. An old man walked by and scowled at Claire. Hillary stepped in front of him and nodded approval at her daughter's Love is Love selection.

This morning, sunlight streamed through the patio doors into the dining room and cast a golden finish on the Italian provincial table and credenza. Italian. So beautiful. After the Pride parade here at home, they'd fly to New York, then to Rome.

Hillary concentrated on the coming week. Claire

was eager to march with her friends to the state capitol. Hillary blew on her coffee as her husband Ed scanned the news on his iPad. He let out a low whistle, his jade green eyes narrowed to slits, and handed the device across the table to her.

The *Sacramento Bee* headline blared: Local Anti-LGBTQ Crimes Doubled

As Hillary glanced through the story, a bolt of fear shot through her. She gave back the iPad and said, "There's supposed to be good security on the parade route, yes?" She dragged her fingers through her hair, twisted it into a loose bun and stabbed it in place with her favorite tortoise shell hair pin.

Ed shook his head and turned to pull a small cigar from a box on the credenza. "I'll be working security at the arena. I won't be able to keep an eye on the parade."

Claire waltzed in through the dining room archway, sporting her new Love is Love tee shirt and denim skirt stamped with a huge rainbow. "How do I look?" She spread her arms and gave a twirl, slowed by her cork-soled walking sandals.

Hillary smiled. "Beautiful."

"What do you mean, Dad, keep an eye on the parade?" At the credenza, Claire slipped a pod into the Nespresso machine and hit the start button.

"You know, for any haters that might want to rain on the parade." He rolled the little cigar back and forth, clamped it unlit between his teeth, and spoke around the cigar. "City cops are all in. They should handle any clashes." He took the cigar out and pointed it at Hillary. "Your mother will be there, too. She's put away a few bad dudes in her day."

Claire frowned. "My squad doesn't need babysitting."

Hillary's stomach clenched. Claire was naive. She'd been so protected.

Ed tapped his iPad. "Hate crime's up lately. Doesn't hurt to be prepared, daughter."

Claire fluffed her short blond hair, so it stood out in soft curls. "Okay, I'm petite for a point guard, but good at karate, better than Mom. Just worry about *her*."

Hillary choked on her coffee, sputtered, and pressed her napkin against her lips.

"We line up before the parade in that same place as last year, right, Mom?" Claire blew on her Cappuccino.

It took Hillary a couple seconds to catch her breath before she answered. "Yes. Southside Park, near the freeway, but keep alert, know who's near you. It isn't so much the homeless in the park as those so-called Christians marching up and down with signs saying 'LGBTQ = End Time Abomination.'"

Claire laughed. "Don't be gloomy, Mom. The parade's going to be fun. And next week's good times in New York. Paisley's coming, isn't she?"

Hillary looked at Ed.

He gave a slight nod and said, "I hope so, honey. Your grandmother is excited about seeing the

Metropolitan Museum of Art. But her plans aren't certain yet."

Hillary cleared her throat. "I'd love it to be just the three of us getting away together." She smiled at her daughter. "The way we used to."

Claire wrinkled her nose. "What's with you, Mom? Of course, Paisley's coming," she said brightly. "Who wouldn't want to go to New York and Italy?"

Hillary worked to keep her expression neutral.

Claire downed her coffee in a few swallows. "Have to go change. Basketball practice at 10:00. Got to try out my new Nikes." She dashed out and down the hall.

Hillary glared at Ed. "I wish you'd support me on this." She clenched her fist and set it next to her coffee mug. "Paisley's keeping us guessing. It's selfish of her making me wait to make reservations."

"I know, but your mixed message is confusing for Claire."

Hillary bounced her fist on the tabletop, and said, "This is my summer break. I deserve to have some fun."

"Hey, Professor." Ed put his unlit cigar back into the box and reached across the table. "When you rescued your mother and brought her here, you signed up for this."

"Paisley owes me an apology." Hillary clenched her jaw.

"You know Paisley's not the apologizing kind."

Hillary sipped at her Intenso and tried to swallow

her anger. "Putting up with her has been more than I imagined."

"Like I've been more than you imagined from back when that butcher was cutting up managers in the superstore?" He took her hand, opened her fist and bent to kiss her palm.

"Mmmmm," she murmured, rocking side to side. "My detective partner. What we've been through."

Claire yelled goodbye and slammed shut the front door.

Ed planted little kisses along the inside of Hillary's arm and whispered, "And more to come, Genevieve."

There it was. His pet name for her. Hillary let go her hurt and anger. She melted into the warm summer morning, alone in the house with Ed. Her rock.

2
FATHER TOMMASO

Valdos Verde, a village northeast of Rome, Italy

Father Tommaso rubbed the cedar rail at the top of the pulpit and gazed out over the nave of Santa Maria. Not many candles had been lit in the colored glass votives in the candle stand. Sunlight streamed through the stained-glass windows and lit up the faithful parishioners. Fewer each week. Got to get the fallen-away back to Mass. Respecting tradition.

There was Mary in the front pew, her green blouse falling off her shoulders, locks of her black hair teasing her neckline. As he frowned, Mary seemed to morph into an image of his mother—her face made up and ready to stroll the street. A trickle of sweat made its way down the small of his back.

Tradition. His mother had refused to respect it. Tommaso blinked away her image. All women should cherish tradition. If he had become a Bishop, he would have helped to hold the line.

Clutching the rail to divert his attention from the tendrils of a headache, he cleared his throat and began his homily. "We read today of the fallen woman, Mary Magdalene. A sinner saved by our Lord. How many among you need that redeeming grace?" He looked at Mary and the stranger sitting by her, shoulder to shoulder. Mary lifted her penciled eyebrows, smiled at him and nudged the other woman.

He notched up his volume. "Look around you. How many are as modest, humble and obedient as our Holy Mother? Not many, and why is that? I'll tell you why. The devil himself has latched on to women, driving them to claim rights and run for political office. To want power in the church. St. Paul tells us a woman's place is to be quiet. God tells them to be a helpmate. And yet, women want to be rulers."

Tommaso paused, taking a few breaths. "Worst of all, some are publicly demanding to become ordained." He pounded the railing. "Ordained to the priesthood!" He surveyed the thirty or so in the sanctuary of his parish church. More than half were shaking their heads. They were right to be dismayed.

"Yes! Shake your heads! Jesus Christ chose twelve disciples. All men. Tasked to carry the good news and forgive sins." He paused.

"Pope Benedict excommunicated the Danube Seven because those women refused to repent for their heretical offense. They had no right to receive Holy Orders nor did that bishop to ordain them." Some eyes opened wider as he grew louder. He knew he was shouting, but it was the right tactic.

Mary and her friend glanced at each other, a smirk on their red lips. His wool garments clung to his damp skin. A few of the old men mopped their foreheads with handkerchiefs on this hot Sunday morning.

Others nodded, and not just the old gray beards, but two of the young married couples, as well. Tommaso directed his remarks toward them. "Wives, desire your husband and his rule over you, as God told Eve in Genesis 3.16."

Tommaso glared at Mary and that woman, waving black silk fans in front of their made-up faces. "Unmarried women and widows, keep your chastity guarded, and your hearts humble in the service of God and your neighbors."

He hadn't seen Mary in the confessional box for months and wondered if he should even serve her and her friend communion. He swiped at a trail of perspiration along his brow.

After kissing the altar table, backing up and bowing before it, Tommaso led the way out of the sanctuary. His headache throbbing under the sun's glare, he stood on the broad top step, ignoring the occasional twinge of pain in his legs, shaking hands with parishioners.

Mary and her friend were among the last to leave. Tommaso gave Mary a firm handshake and said, "You do know when confession hours are, Mary?"

She shrugged her shoulders, her sleeves inching down. "Indeed, I do. But I don't know why you focus on a fallen Mary Magdalen. You know the church has admitted its error of seeing her as a prostitute."

Tommaso's face matched the red bougainvillea climbing the front wall of the church. "I was making a moral point, not a literal statement."

"And," Mary's friend interjected, "the Apostles were jealous of her relationship with Jesus, so they started that slur against her character."

Tommaso scowled. "My job is to look out for *your* character, dear ladies."

He nodded at a married couple passing by whom he'd sent to a counselor last year. When the wife turned her head and called out to their young son, her husband leered at Mary's friend. Tommaso suspected that Mary's blonde friend was a troublemaker of the first order.

A boy ran towards the couple, yelling, "Wait for me!" Tommaso turned to Mary. "And whom have you brought to Mass today?'

Mary slipped her arm around her friend's waist. "My college roommate, Delilah, visiting from California."

Tommaso nodded. He pointed to a sign by the sun-bleached cypress doors and said in ringing tones, "Confession hours are posted there. I hope to see you both before next Sunday."

"Oh, Father," Mary said sweetly, "next Sunday, we'd love a homily about Marina the Monk. Her feast day is soon." She hooked arms with her friend, and they sashayed down the worn steps and out toward the village square.

It struck Tommaso that today might be a good day to take the pulse of the village, go for a caffè at Giulia's.

BACK INSIDE THE CHURCH, TOMMASO PASSED BY THE confessional and ran his hand over the dark wood of the cabinet. For a split second, he let himself imagine Mary's confession, the intimacy in the stall with the filigree pass-through window.

Up front, his head throbbing, he stared at the ornamented sides of the pulpit. Last month, the carved Green Man mask had been unfastened and stolen. His shoulders sagged.

He rubbed his fingertips along the fabric of his stole. He had failed to build up the church, not even his small corner of it. And now, he didn't even have the Green Man to gaze at for consolation. When men were fruitful. That fantasy floated through his mind, his secret sin, the legend of seeds planted below

Adam's tongue by his son Seth, shooting forth and bringing new life.

Sometimes the Green Man had looked like he was grinning. Other times, as if tormented. Of course, this was not Church dogma. Tommaso faced Christ on the cross, hanging behind the altar, and cried, "Forgive Me!"

In the cool, dark vestry, he lifted off his stole, green for Ordinary Time. He snorted. These times were hardly ordinary. Mary and her friend were standout examples, led on by left-wing politicians. Something had to be done. The Cardinal was right.

In the canonica's kitchen, he made himself a lunch of bread and cheese, took it out to his office and set it on his desk. He scrolled through his email. Vito had sent him an article advocating therapists and priests working together to heal the broken. It warned of a Jesuit who worked alone exorcizing a demon and got sent to an insane asylum for the rest of his life. It was safer to work alongside others. That Vito. Good man. Doing God's work.

Tommaso made the sign of the cross, said a quick prayer, and forced himself to take a bite of bread. His appetite was not what it was before. He prayed those injections had been in time to halt the progression.

Last month, Tommaso had visited the Cardinal to make his annual confession. Sweating profusely, Tommaso had spilled his desires, doubts, and fears, along with his sins—the ones he was willing to reveal.

After Tommaso's confession, the Cardinal took him to his private office. He sat side by side with Tommaso and handed him a box of tissues to wipe the sweat from his face. "Banish your doubts, Tommaso. You are not alone. Our Pope will soon speak in public alongside our new premier Meloni. They will urge Italian women to have more children, to reverse our record low birth rate. Our Holy Father supports concrete action to halt our 'demographic winter.' He believes something can still be done to reverse the trend."

The Cardinal bent closer to Tommaso. "But I fear our Pope is not doing enough. I have a project in mind and an important role for you to play."

Tommaso listened with care as the Cardinal laid out his vision and the assistance he prayed that Tommaso would render. "I want you, Tommaso, to lead this return to the Father."

"I can't do that, your excellency. I am old and sick," Tommaso said.

"You look at the peak of health!"

"Looks can be deceiving. I'm suffering from a disease I should have treated years ago, but pride got in my way."

"I will be at your side. You will not take on this sacred task alone." The Cardinal rose and dipped his head, signaling the discussion was completed.

The Cardinal had shared his plan last week, and Tommaso's trusted friends had accepted the invitation for tomorrow's meeting. A shred of hope pierced

Tommaso's despair, but he was tired. A short nap with no dreams sounded good.

TOMMASO STRETCHED OUT HIS FINGERS TOWARD women in a ring, dancing, circling, laughing. He waggled his fingertips, but the tail end of the dream vanished in the afternoon heat. He blinked his eyes, and his hands trembled. That same old dream. He gazed at the ceiling, gave his head a good shake, and sat up.

A glance at his Samsung told him he'd slept longer than he intended. It was so quiet here. Father Miglio had been transferred last year, not needed for the dwindling numbers here, except on those Sundays when Tommaso was away from the village.

Fiorella, who came every other day to cook and tidy, was not allowed to live here. Some priests craved women, even after ordination. Not Tommaso. He hadn't carried on with anyone after his wild days ended with that call from God. His Father. The only one he knew.

A caffè sounded good. He set out for Giulia's. Hardly anyone was out and about in the square. It was still riposo, quiet time indoors for those blessed to live as families. Giulia reopened her cafe at six for the tourists. Tommaso sat and fed the pigeons until the town clock struck six.

Resisting Giulia's invitation to sit and eat, he stood at the bar and downed a caffè. Giulia was a good mother, her six children grown and living their own lives. Her husband Vincent ran the kitchen.

"Siediti e mangia," she repeated. Tommaso gave in. "Make it a pizzetta, per favore."

She arched her eyebrows. "A small, for you?" She flew her hands in an arc over her ample belly. "No grande?"

"Piccola. Small." He nodded, his lips pursed. "E una birra piccola." Six ounces of beer was all he could handle these days. "Where's Carlo?" he asked. "I have a few things to run by him."

"In Sicily, visiting Nonni," she said. "Can I help you?"

"Ask him to come see me when he gets back, per favore." Giulia's brother was a bit of an il gradasso, showing off or bragging sometimes when keeping a secret was called for, but still, the man was sincere in doing the work of the Father. Tommaso needed to give Carlo a description of that blonde friend visiting Mary.

Tommaso nodded toward a door in the far corner. "What's going on lately?"

Giulia laughed. "Just the usual festa di compleanno, celebrating birthdays." She called out Tommaso's order into the kitchen and went to welcome tourists starting to filter in.

Tommaso noticed two young women dressed in rainbow tee shirts, holding hands and nuzzling each other right there in the dining room. He looked away, his face flushed, a silent prayer in his heart, for their guidance.

Within minutes, Giulia set down a large Margherita Pizza. "Buon appetito."

Tommaso groaned. "Grazia." He couldn't refuse Giulia's generosity. She never let him pay for anything, counted it as part of her offerings to the Lord.

BACK AT THE CANONICA, TOMMASO SAT ON THE OLD divan in front of the TV. His stomach churned and rumbled. Too much pizza. He felt worse as he watched the news. A group of skimpily dressed women, calling themselves sex workers, marched through the street, holding red umbrellas over their heads and banners demanding better treatment, health benefits. Red umbrellas.

His eyes glazed over, and his mind receded into childhood. Red stockings, black leather miniskirts, his mother's friends out in the street tickling him, chanting, "Tesoruccio," little treasure, until he fell down, laughing so hard he wet his pants.

His mother hauling him up the stairs and throwing him down onto a pile of dirty clothes covering his blanket. "Avrei dovuto sbarazzarmi di te! I should have got rid of you!" She ran out and left him alone in the apartment, shivering in his wet clothes and crying himself to sleep.

The next morning, there she was, dragging him by

the hand to church, lighting a candle in front of the statue of the Virgin, and asking the priest to bless them both. But each night, she was back out on the street. He was alone in the dirty apartment.

The TV blared on, the sex worker women voicing their grievances. "What about your children?" Tommaso whispered.

He bent and cupped his cheeks in his hands, holding back unshed tears.

3
HILLARY

Today, Hillary had to ask her mother for a favor. She didn't want to, but the *Sacramento Bee* article had warned crime against gays was increasing. Claire was downtown at the arena for a noontime summer youth basketball event where Ed was supervising security. Now was the time.

Hillary stepped out onto the decomposed granite path, fortified by crunching sounds underfoot. Her view of their well-kept back yard soothed her nerves. The lawn was a lush green, so different from that weedy patch she remembered from childhood. In those days before her mother was gone, she would come flying out of her studio and tackle Hillary, pulling her down onto the grass.

"Yellow flowers in your red hair, my favorite colors," her mother would shout. "All colors are beautiful." She would launch into "I Can Sing a Rainbow" while braiding a circlet of dandelions. Hillary would sit frozen in place until her mother pressed the floppy tiara on top of Hillary's head. "Now you are queen, silly dilly!" She would pinch Hillary's cheeks, then jump up and run back into her studio.

Hillary hated how the weeds got her hair all matted. She wished her mother would comb it and clip it back with a barrette like Suzy's, so smooth and tidy. Hillary would work the circlet loose and place it near the walnut tree. Once back in her room, she would brush her hair until it felt glossy again.

Out on the velvet lawn this morning, a newly sprung chickweed blossom caught Hillary's eye. She bent to examine the tiny white flower, pinch it out and put it in her pocket, prevent it from multiplying into a nuisance. She continued walking toward the cottage they'd had built for her mother a couple years back, after Hillary rescued her from the life of a street artist in San Francisco, at the mercy of whoever would give her shelter.

She didn't want to ask Paisley for anything, but the Pride parade might bring out the haters. In the past, Hillary had stopped people from hurting Claire. But this was different. Hillary fingered the tiny Mary medal hanging from her black bead bracelet.

It shouldn't be that hard to ask her mother for this, easier than asking for what she really wanted. Hillary stamped her soles hard against the gritty pathway underfoot.

She knocked softly on the cottage door and waited, then knocked again, and waited. She walked around behind the cottage and checked to be sure Paisley's car was parked in the alley before she went back and knocked again.

A few minutes later, Paisley opened the door. "I'm busy," she said, stabbing the air with an 8-inch paint brush, making her look taller and bigger than her petite self—her halo of white hair streaked with blue made her look like she stepped out of a painting herself.

"I've come to ask for a few hours of your time." Hillary tried to keep a pleasant expression on her face. "Not today." She added, "Not until next Saturday. To help me protect Claire in the parade."

Her mother turned to an easel that took up most of the tiny room's space. She narrowed her eyes at the ocean sunset she was painting and glanced down at a card showing a similar scene, resting on the easel's ledge. "You know I despise crowds," she said.

Hillary worked to keep herself from whining. "This is not exactly a crowd. It's more of a celebration that supports your granddaughter. You love her, I know."

"I love the individual she is. Not the group you claim she's part of." Paisley dabbed at a blob of yellow on her pallet.

Hillary moved near the easel so she could face her mother. "The problem is that hate crimes are rising, and Ed can't be with us at the parade. If you come along, I won't look so much like a helicopter mother."

"So, you want me to act out a lie." Paisley brushed on yellow paint near the horizon line.

There it was. All the focus on herself. No interest in protecting her granddaughter. "Sticking together for safety is not a lie," Hillary said.

"I live with integrity," Paisley said. "To thine own self be true. The Bard's plays were not written by committee, were they!"

"The parade will only last a few hours," Hillary said. "It'll be along that same route you marched in the 60s, against the war." Hillary clasped her hands together and raised them as if carrying an invisible protest sign. "Remember how you were part of the peace movement?"

Paisley frowned. "Your father isolated me, stuck me home alone with you." Paisley poked her brush into the black paint on her pallet. "I'm just fine here."

"So, the hell with everyone else? Now you abandon your granddaughter? Like you abandoned me back then?" Hillary was shouting.

Paisley stabbed the black paint. "You were not left alone." Her tone took on a loud, slow cadence. "I stayed until you were ten. The Bronte sisters lost their mother at that age and look what they achieved." Paisley streaked black paint across the sandy beach, below the setting sun. "Claire will be fine in the parade. You'll see to it."

Hillary held her fists clenched down at her sides. "You're nothing but a narcissist, running out on Claire now, like you ran out on me."

Paisley smiled as she feathered the edges of black into the blue of the sea. "I'm not running out. I just learned I've been accepted into the artists' colony in Venice. I'll be coming along on your trip. That will be more than enough time for us all to be together."

"I can't believe you!" Hillary tore out of the tiny house and raced down the pathway, her feet beating faster than her pounding heart. On the patio steps, she sat in a shady patch and bent over to catch her breath. She fingered the butterfly tattoo on her ankle. How could she stand flying away for the summer with that selfish woman?

She drove to the dojo and went through the afternoon strength practice even though it was Sunday, and she'd been there three times last week, the first full week of her summer vacation from teaching at Clearwater College.

4
FATHER TOMMASO

Tommaso fingered a bump at the side of his jaw as he steered his old Fiat 500 over the road lined with Cypress trees. He got to Pisano in half an hour, but even here, in the noonday sun of this little village, women in shorts paraded their bodies. Two of them in the street waved purple silk scarves at him and forced him to veer to avoid hitting them. He held his temper, but the in-your-face aspect of the problem seemed to be growing worse all the time.

Parking was at a premium, now that Osteria Cantoro was listed by Gayot among the top 10 restaurants in Tuscany. He had to take a spot a couple blocks away. The heat of early summer pressed him to hurry along, dressed as he was in his black wool suit, although shooting pains in his legs slowed him down. Inside, the beefy aroma of Bistecca on the grill filled him with cheer. Food. Tradition. It mattered.

Pressing his fingertips just below the white band of his Roman collar, he threaded past tables crowded with chattering tourists. He watched for recognition, but no one gave him even a nod. His cheeks grew flushed.

Tall, thin Pietro stood at the back of the restaurant, tending Bistecca sizzling over charcoal flames. Tommaso's mood brightened as he stopped to admire Pietro slapping herbs tied in twine over the butter-basted steaks.

"We're all set to feed your guests," Pietro said. Tommaso smiled. His mouth watered as he left by the door in the far corner. He scanned the narrow passage ahead. It wasn't easy to navigate tight places like this, with his vision dimming. After proceeding ten feet, he leaned against the rough stone wall and assessed his balance. He studied the scene from the top of the staircase, overjoyed at the sight of these friends who'd accepted his invitation to come discuss the problem.

The absence of hand railings made him set down his foot with care before taking each step as he lowered himself down the stairs, fanning open to a broad clearing in the cellar. Flickering light from wall sconces illuminated the ancient room. Beyond the clearing, tunnels stretched like spokes of a broken wheel, disappearing into the earthy darkness. On plank shelves lay bottles of wine, wheels of cheese and jugs of olive oil.

Tommaso sucked in his cheeks and inhaled the

earthy aromas. Soon, women would be coming to serve them. Bottles of Chianti stood on the long table near bowls of plump strawberries and golden grapes. Not much bruschetta was left. Tommaso's stomach growled. He would wait until after he gave the blessing to bite into the grilled bread, sprinkled with the freshest chopped tomatoes, olive oil and a little salt.

He nodded at Roger, seated at the head of the table. The American media mogul called out, "Buongiorno, Father!" Roger held his arms up as if to catch something falling from the sky. "Spirito Santo burns here." The others around the table raised their arms and waved their hands as if their fingers were flames.

"Fire preserves unity," called out the Cardinal, dressed in a black cassock, his scarlet sash at a diagonal across his chest. Heartened by the Cardinal's confidence in him, Tommaso had given these men the bare outline of the problem the Cardinal wanted addressed. And here they were, gathered to reason together. Tommaso bowed in the Cardinal's direction and took the seat left open for him at Roger's right hand.

Roger addressed the men. "The sparse attendance in Florence last Sunday at Pentecost has showcased the problem. Our churches have become tourist attractions, museums. We need them to return to centers of living faith that strengthens the nation. The time for fire is …."

He fell silent as a woman appeared at the top of

the stairs, her arms laden with plates. The fragrance of sage and garlic filled the air. A couple of helpers followed, similarly burdened. The three of them descended the steps of the fan-shaped stairway. The men leaned back to make room for glistening steaks and bowls of creamy white beans to be set before them.

Tommaso's heart swelled at the women, going about their service with modest grace. When the women left, Tommaso cleared his throat and offered a prayer. "Father, stoke the flames of desire within the hearts of the faithful to return our country to you. Help us live as imitatores Dei Patris. Bless this food as strength for our mission. We ask this in the name of Jesus. Amen."

Roger sliced off a corner of his steak and thrust it into his mouth. He chewed vigorously and swallowed. With a quick nod, he said, "Buon Appetito!" The men cut into their meat, and silence reigned, broken by moans of pleasure.

After they devoured their meal, Roger took a strawberry from the bowl. "Siamo alla frutta," he said and sliced off the top of the red berry, placing the green stem on the edge of his plate. "We're at the fruit, the end of the meal." He made two bites of the berry, wiped his mouth with his napkin and scooted back, his chair scraping on the stone floor. "Let's consider the problem Father Tommaso has brought to our attention: the infectious uprising of women, causing chaos in our time." He stood, stretching his five-foot-six-inch frame.

Roger's glance touched the face of each man before he went on. "In America, the church is fighting to protect the unborn and to return women to their place in the family. Georgia Meloni is on the same track here, plus worldwide Catholic radio is having an impact. But a few months ago, Elly Schlein was elected and now leads the leftists here in Italy. It is a sign the peril is growing worse." He nodded at a square-jawed, big-boned man seated across the table from him. "Vito knows from his own experience."

Vito frowned and ran his fingers through his dark brown hair. "Even my own Joleen—" he started coughing. No one said a word as he coughed, tears running down his cheeks.

Tommaso burned with sympathetic humiliation over what his friend had endured this past year. Vito's wife had taken their young children and moved to Venice with her lover.

Vito wiped his face with a napkin and managed a sip of water. "She filed." Vito's voice was hoarse. "For separation. After all these years! She's a Catholic, mother of our six children. Da non crederci!"

The Cardinal shook his head. "Women are craving power all over the world. A half million faithful in Brazil burned a witch who was destroying the family. I fear even our beloved Pope is giving in to 'the church of nice.' He's invited women to vote at our Bishops meeting, to advise his Holiness—for the first time ever." He pursed his lips.

Joy flooded Tommaso at the leadership of the Cardinal, one of Italy's most influential advocates for traditional values—values that anyone with eyes to see and ears to hear could realize were slipping away.

The Cardinal continued, "And this Pope is letting a commission on ordaining women deacons move forward, as well. When you think of the global threat, does Brazil's witch burning seem excessive?"

Candlelight and shadows flickered across the faces of those at the table. "Begging your pardon, Excellency," said a slim, bald man, "but it wasn't a real witch burning. They dressed an effigy, clothed her as a witch, and burnt the straw figure. Still, the people were trying to fight evil. We could consider setting effigies on fire. Then we could avoid being sinners ourselves, you know."

Tommaso respected Frank, a Medieval Studies scholar, but he had to correct the man. "It's no sin to combat the devil, Professor."

Frank nodded. "Many women today link arms with the devil and dance themselves into the Inferno. First…" He raised his index finger. "They are wanton with sexuality. Second, they are ambitious in politics and the church. Third, they promote killing with abortion!" He pointed at the Cardinal, and said in a low and solemn tone, "They are like the witches of old. Confession could save their souls."

The Cardinal patted his chest as he leaned

forward, rocking slowly, his brown eyes turning nearly black. "Yes. We are trying to stop them from infecting each other," he said. "The devil makes use of a witch, not because he has need of any such, but because he seeks her eternal punishment and damnation." He got red in the face. "Absolution after Confession could save the precious souls of these women."

Tommaso flushed at the mention of the sacrament. He pictured parishioners lined up at his confessional stall, where he spent time hearing their intimate details, his arousal unobserved.

Roger nodded. "Che Puzza. The extent of the peril stands clear. The church is too soft on the fallen away. Women long for men who are 'chips off the old block' of fatherly love. Now we, with God's help, are called to lead a return to tradition."

Pietro had come down the stairs and joined the group. "Return to tradition! I'm good at getting attention, look at the way the restaurant is thriving. It's hard to find parking anymore." He grinned. "We've started a *Daily Bread* podcast and are using social media. How about a 'Pride in Traditional Family' rally at the Coliseum? Or the Trevi?"

The Cardinal frowned and said, "Those places are tributes to pagan gods. We don't want to hold a rally in St. Peter's Square, either. Could be taken the wrong way."

Tommaso noticed no one was saying what they all knew. There would not be enough people to gather for a rally, if recent church attendance was any measure. The Gay Pride Parade was next week and would make any rally of theirs look pathetic by comparison.

He waited. Candlelight flickering from the sconces cast shadows on the stone walls.

Vito cleared his throat. "I say, let's choose a fallen soul and save her with my therapy. Share her testimony with others. Return to tradition."

A hush fell over the room.

Vito turned to Tommaso and continued, "Your parishioners have benefitted from my HypnoConvert process. It's legal here in Italy. We should use it."

Tommaso considered the parishioners he had sent Vito for counseling. Especially the two young women with homosexual inclinations. They each were married to men now and had children on the way.

Pietro's face paled. "What do you mean 'choose' a fallen soul? You're not suggesting 'kidnap,' are you?"

"Not kidnap, certainly not for ransom," Vito said. "Just select to convert and save their souls."

"Select? Better make sure to get their permission, first," said Pietro.

"Let's all think and pray about this opportunity, and regroup soon to make specific plans," said Tommaso. He was gratified to see looks of enthusiasm on his friends' faces. "One of the spiritual works of mercy is showing sinners the path to salvation," he added.

Vito threw his shoulders back and stood. "In my online coaching, I found some young men who have promise. I'd like to check them out in person, see if they align with us. If they do, I want to invite them to our next meeting, with your permission, Father Tommaso."

Tommaso glanced at the Cardinal, spotted his slight nod of approval, and reached for the nearest bowl of strawberries. He selected a ripe one and bit into the meaty fruit, ignoring the juice dripping from his fingertips. "Yes, Vito," he said. "We need the young and strong—if they are the right kind."

5
SISTER FREDERICKA

Fredericka declined Mother Catherine's invitation to take a cookie. There was less than an hour before Mass. Several times, Fredericka had held forth on the importance of fasting before Holy Communion, but Mother Catherine had her own ideas. Although no one talked about it, all the nuns at Casa di San Carlotta held their own firm convictions, and not all of them aligned with Holy Mother Church dogma.

Today, young Sister Anna was disturbed. "Those people say they're overriding tradition and taking the church to what Jesus really wanted." She tucked a wayward wisp of hair under the bandeau lying flat her forehead. "But, it's what's wrong all over the world, all this support for ..." She raised her eyes to the cross on the wall behind Mother Catherine's desk.

"Support for... For what?" coaxed Catherine.

"You know. Letting it be all right to kill the

unborn, to spill seed onto…" She blushed, the freckles across her face turning into rosy pinpoints.

"Humpf. You've been listening to the old sisters too much. Spilling seed. Happens every night in their dreams. No way to control that, is there now." Mother Catherine finished her cookie, one from a batch she'd baked early this morning. As she brushed one hand against the other, a few crumbs fell on her desk blotter. "Just like I can't control where these crumbs land. Lusting for control is all it is. The whole history of the church. Control us women, and any wayward men—"

Father Bingham burst into Catherine's office. "—wayward men? Looks more like wayward women, late for Communion again. Reverend Mother, this is no way to run a convent."

Mother Catherine stood tall. "Check your watch. You're early, Father." She sailed out of her office, leading the way down the corridor through the foyer to the chapel.

Fredericka gestured for Father Bingham to go first. Such courtesy was due the visiting priest assigned to perform the Divine Service on Tuesdays, after his Sunday duties were over. But his presence vexed her soul. The five remaining members of their order could do it themselves, if the Vatican didn't insist it had no authority to confer ordination on women.

In the chapel, Fredericka lit the single candle on a stand at the side of the altar. Mother Catherine bowed toward the crucifix hanging on the back wall before she crossed in front of the altar to the ambry.

She took out the ciborium and placed it on the altar. "If you could consecrate a few extra wafers, Father, we are running low for some of the homeless who've been asking for communion."

He glared at her. "You're not serving the host to just anyone who drops by for a handout, are you? How can you know if they are in good standing?"

"Our Lord never asked about good standing, now did he?" Mother Catherine set the metal ciborium down next to the wafers and the chalice of wine that the priest was about to consecrate.

Fredericka wouldn't dream of telling Father Bingham that Mother had occasionally blessed bread she'd baked in the convent oven and used it for the poor souls who needed not just a meal but something to hold body and soul together. Father Bingham would report Mother to the Bishop.

None of the Casa di San Carlotta sisters were ready for consequences from veering off the straight and narrow. Fredericka knew some things needed to be kept secret until the time was right. She was preparing her mind and body to face any repercussions. Or suffering. If she had to.

6

XAVIER

To escape the afternoon heat, Xavier waited in the church for Vito. He stared at the fresco of the three women tied to a post, flames licking at their long gowns. It was like that book cover from childhood. Last week, some guy in incels.co had posted he wished he could burn the bitch at his gym who wouldn't smile back at him.

Xavier studied the faded work of art. Wild grape vines had crept up through cracks in the church's stone floor and covered a few orange flames with tiny green leaves. He turned to scan the empty nave, its thick stone walls lined with crypts of village leaders, laid to rest over the centuries. He kept an eye on the open space where the wooden front doors had fallen away.

The five acres of Sangiovese vines had dried into skeletal branches, woven around rusty wires nailed to the trellises. Guilt warmed Xavier's cheeks. Father Joseph was no longer alive to haul the thick hoses around, water the grapes. Xavier's slender frame was not capable of such a burdensome task. He had tried, and failed. Just like he failed at most things.

Xavier had risen before dawn and baked bread in the abbey's clay oven using Father Joseph's old method. Not in holiday shapes like the ones that mysteriously arrived for him on Easter and Christmas. But edible. He'd toasted it into bruschetta to serve Vito. Xavier had grown to trust Vito, a professional who coached men who wanted a romantic partner but were unable to get one. When Vito had texted and asked to come talk to Albert and him, Xavier was excited. When Vito arrived, he'd take him down below, and the three of them could talk. In private. They would be even more secluded than in an online forum.

Shafts of light filtered in through stained glass windows. Xavier wiped his forehead with the rumpled sleeve of his white shirt. A sudden shift of the flat stones under his feet made Xavier shield his eyes and look up through the shallow-pitched terra cotta roofing. Minor earthquakes had tweaked open bits of the nave's ceiling to the sky. Nothing was moving except dust motes in the afternoon heat. Italy sat on several fault lines, Xavier reminded himself. This was just normal fault creep.

It looked like Vito might be later than what he'd

said. Few people realized how hard the climb was, up the long hillside from Voce Sotto to the monastery or even that the monastery still stood. The Church had given up on the abbey decades ago, since so few men became monks anymore, and old Father Joseph was left on his own to tend the place.

Xavier had cared for Father Joseph in his last months. Now, it was better than when he was a child, an orphan here. He had a new friend. A friend who didn't make fun of him and his weak chin. He'd got to know Albert online, and today, Albert was down below. And Vito was coming to talk to the two of them. Xavier felt as close to smiling as he'd ever come.

"Buongiorno!" A booming voice shook him from his reverie. "You must be Xavier, yes?"

Standing in the opening left by the missing doors, the bulk of the man was compelling—over six feet tall, dark brown hair, eyes to match. In a light blue shirt and tan trousers, Vito held a striped jacket slung over his shoulder, hooked by his index finger. Xavier had never seen Vito in person, only his profile pic in the forum chat room. Xavier swallowed his initial shock like a large pill. Vito was a classic Chad, a magazine model, a sexually desirable alpha male. But of course. Vito was an expert on getting women to fall into his arms. That's why he was a dating coach. Xavier trusted the man, after all they had shared online.

"Vito!" Xavier went to Vito and reached up to embrace him, kissing him on both cheeks. Xavier stepped back. "Let's go down into the catacomb, and you can meet Albert in the flesh."

Vito flashed a bright smile. "Lead the way."

Xavier went to a table in the transverse chapel and palmed a small oil lamp. "We use these when we're on the stairs. The power was shut off after Father Joseph died, and the bills didn't get paid anymore."

Vito gave him a quick, sidelong glance. "How do you get online?"

"We charge our devices in the village." Xavier handed the lamp to Vito. "Father Joseph had us make these out of clay, in the abbey workroom. They're better than candles on the stairs, but keep it level, so the oil doesn't spill."

He lit Vito's lamp and one for himself, then he opened a black, wrought-iron door. "This heavy door keeps it cool down there." He stepped onto a landing, at the top of an old stairwell and waved Vito to follow him. The door closed behind them with a loud smack.

"It's dark here, but it'll be light down below. Workers cut shafts from the surface. When the digging was finished, the shafts were kept open for ventilation and lighting."

Xavier pressed a palm against the earthen wall and with his other hand held the oil lamp to illuminate the stairs. He stepped with care onto the long stairwell.

"It has that dank smell like in old churches," Vito observed, his voice loud behind Xavier.

Xavier glanced over his shoulder at Vito. "Don't worry, there is plenty of good air, not dangerous like the deep tunnels at St. Sebastian's."

"Back in my school days, we toured St. Sebastian's catacombs," Vito said. "Lots of the niches there were empty. Grave robbers. Have you got empty ones?"

"Several, yes."

"I'm thinking they could be outfitted to work as berths."

"Berths?"

"You know, like on train cars, but for people to rest during a retreat."

It sounded weird to Xavier, and he said, "I don't know about using the niches that way."

"The cellar my friends meet in has lower floors, but it's not used for burials or berths. Just for wine," Vito said.

Xavier took the last step and turned to check on Vito. "After we go through the passage ahead, we'll come to a clearing. We won't need these lamps. We've put in battery-powered LED lights."

"Enterprising," Vito said.

"It's an open, lighted spacc with a room behind it, for funeral and memorial services."

Xavier led the way along the dim passage, pointing out empty coffin-sized shelves dug into the earthen walls of the tunnel. In respect for the people stolen from their resting places, Xavier spoke softly as he walked on.

"The niches with covers still in place hold bodies that were wrapped in a sheet, like our Lord. Then the resting place was sealed with clay tile and a little marker attached." He pointed. "See? Their names were carved into small tiles before baking."

"I see crosses carved, too," Vito said. "All Christians in these crypts, right?"

"Supposed to be," Xavier responded. "But Father Joseph said the word 'crypt' comes from the Greek and means 'hidden.' Only God knows what was hidden in their hearts." He smiled. "For Father Joseph himself, I used an empty niche, ahead near the clearing. Laid his body in there. He was like a father to me. By the end, he'd shrunk to skin over bones, so I carried him here myself and got him sealed up."

Vito grunted. "Isn't the Vatican concerned over the situation? Not knowing what all is going on inside their property?"

"They can't keep up with so many abandoned monasteries, some nearly covered with vines, so they're left to wither away. We get ignored. I like it that way," Xavier said. "Soon, we'll pass by Father Joseph."

He walked a few steps and stopped to face a bright terra cotta gravestone. "Riposa in pace," he murmured and crossed himself. He looked at Vito.

After Vito repeated his words and actions, Xavier

continued on down the dim tunnel towards the open lighted place.

Xavier set his oil lamp on a rack and motioned for Vito to follow his example. With a candle snuffer, Xavier smothered the flames at the tips of their lamps. He moved over to a long table where a man with a smooth olive complexion and neatly shaped blond eyebrows sat and watched them.

"Vittorio Gallo, meet Albert Crosby," Xavier said, glad he didn't need to give his own last name.

Albert stood to shake hands. "Buonasera, Signore Gallo."

"Call me Vito, per favore."

"And I'm Albert." He flashed a smile.

Xavier pulled out a chair for Vito. "You know from the forums, Albert is an expat American."

Albert grinned. "I'm not for hiding away online but getting out in the world."

Vito cleared his throat. "Tell me what brought you to Italy." He took a small notebook from his jacket pocket.

"I've seen photos of my mother, Teresa. She was a saint, died giving birth to me, thirty-two years ago, today." He made the sign of the cross.

Xavier pushed a plate of bruschetta towards Vito. "Please, have some birthday bruschetta." Vito took a piece and lifted it in a salute to Albert.

Albert nodded somberly and continued. "But my son of a bitch corporate attorney father remarried when I was thirteen. Mariotte, my stepmother." He paused and stared at Vito. "She wanted to be dominated. She trained me when my father was out of town."

Vito nodded, his lips pressed into a tight, straight line.

"It was heaven and hell as I grew, obese and covered with acne. At sixteen, I ran away and worked at an Italian restaurant in New York. Along with growing a big, hooked nose…" He looked at Vito through narrowed eyelids. "I was growing myself a set of man tools, but I had a tough time picking up women. I read books and blogs, watched YouTube, and posted in chat rooms. No luck. I became a head waiter, collected tips to afford plastic surgery and gave myself this look." He thrust out his jaw.

"'Looksmaxxing,'" said Vito, "nothing wrong with looking your best."

The corner of Xavier's lip drooped, and his chin quivered. He pulled at his short beard. Nothing could be done about his face, but he had his new Marcelli sneakers to add a couple inches to his height.

Albert took a deep breath. "Still no luck with women. I dropped a hundred pounds, still nothing. I envied the rep of Italian men as lovers, so I moved over. Still no luck, so I joined pick-up artists forums. And finally, women took to me. But," he scowled, "memories of Mariotte taunting me, calling me Fat Albert, forcing me to slap her around, made me despise the easy pickups, want to punish them, convert them to saintly, like my mother." He made the sign of the cross and kissed his fingertips.

Vito tapped his notebook with his fingertips.

A grin spread across Albert's closely shaved cheeks. "Truth is, they like being raped, even when they're yelling, 'No.' And it's the alpha male path to pleasure."

Vito's eyebrows shot up. "'Alpha male.' What's it mean to you?"

"Chads. Guys that choosy females open their arms to. Men like you, Vito. Square-jawed, big-boned. The kind they want to father their children."

Albert roughed up his blond hair until it was sticking out in all directions. "I fool them, pick 'em up just to slam 'em down. Shame 'em."

"He's good at pickup lines. Not like me." Xavier's chin trembled.

Albert nodded. "When Xavier posted he was fixing up an abandoned monastery, I moved to the village to join him. This is a perfect place to bring 'em, get 'em to confess, practice penance, you could say."

Vito paced the length of the open, lighted place, his brow furrowed. He stopped where a beam of sunlight spilled from a narrow air shaft open to the late afternoon sky. "Penance? Not the fantasy of massacring Chad and Stacy normies, right?" He looked from one to the other. "No mass killings."

"No, not at all. Not into mass anything!" Xavier

held out his hands, palms up as if imploring the divine. "One at a time, be open to loving us."

Vito nodded. "My therapy is to help women return to their God-given roles."

"I've created a special means of persuasion," said Albert. He walked to the shelf holding the oil lamps and picked up a box. "I keep this here, don't want my nosy landlady in the village snooping."

At the table, he opened the box and took out a package of flesh-colored squares. "It's been a long time since I first learned, so I practiced on fake skin before I worked on my buddy."

Vito returned to his chair, his pen lying on the tabletop, the pages of his notebook empty, his eyes wide open, watching Albert.

"Show Vito what you've got," Albert directed Xavier.

Xavier rolled up his long white sleeve to reveal a small black tattoo on his slack bicep.

Vito grunted and said, "Looks like barbed wire."

"It's wires holding grapes on trellises," Xavier said.

Albert nodded and rocked in his chair. "Injections of ink cause a burning sensation and open people up. Under the pen, Xavier told me about living here as an orphan."

Xavier looked down at the cross-hatched lines on his arm and spoke in a husky tone. "Father Joseph was in charge. The vineyard was crowded. Men wore brown robes with white ropes around their middles.

They called each other 'brother.' I called the other orphans 'brother' before they snuck behind me in the rows of grapes and punched me in the back, called me 'pigface.'"

Vito picked up his pen and began writing in his notebook.

"Father Joseph would take me inside, teach me to bake bread in the clay ovens, show me how to read Latin, the lives of the Saints, and the *Malleus* witch book."

Xavier stared at his tattoo and wiped his forehead with the long white sleeve on his other arm. "When the brothers left and took the others with them, I knew I was special, getting to stay with Father Joseph." He gazed in the direction of the tunnel where the old priest was entombed.

He turned to look at Albert. "Albert feels like a real brother. Not like my mother who abandoned me here." His lip quivered. "I must have been ugly. But she didn't abort me." Tears glistened in his dark brown eyes.

He rolled down his sleeve. "Women love Chads. I want some kind of miracle to change them. Albert likes to punish them first."

Albert reached into the box again, took out a bottle of ink, and wagged it in Vito's direction. "Tattoos punish and persuade at the same time. I use black ink and a pen machine that runs on batteries."

Vito nodded. "I see." He looked around the room. "Are there provisions for a lengthy stay here?"

"We haven't stayed overnight, but we could if we brought bedding for the niches," Albert said.

"We've got some things," Xavier said. He led Vito back to the other room. "There's an altar where people used to say prayers for the dead," Xavier said. "We fit in a new Boxio portable toilet and sink set up." He pumped the foot pedal to show Vito how the water ran out into the low box of a sink. Xavier raised a half-full gallon jug. "Albert hauls up water from the village. Want a drink?"

Vito shook his head and said, "No, but I'll have another piece of your birthday bruschetta." He walked back into the open lighted place.

Vito finished up his bruschetta and smiled. "It was good to meet you in person, both of you. I think we may be able to help each other." He looked up at the shaft open to the sky. Sunlight dimmed from a passing cloud. "Dei Patris aims for spiritual transformation for lost souls."

"Women's souls, yes?" asked Xavier.

Vito nodded and stood. "I'm inviting you to our meeting tomorrow. I'll text you the details." He shook his head, his lip twisted down on one side. "I need to leave now. My oldest daughter is expecting me for dinner, to console me for her mother running off to Venice."

Xavier lit two oil lamps, gave one to Vito and led the way back down the dark tunnel passage, up the stairs and out into the empty church. As they passed the fresco of the women standing in the fire, Xavier pointed to the flames. "I don't think it will take that to convert them."

"Please, God, no burnings," said Vito.

Xavier walked Vito to the corner of the rows of dead vines and watched him start down the hillside. The pink light of evening bathed the vines, and Xavier felt a surge of hope that new life could be coming.

7
FATHER TOMMASO

Tommaso rested his elbow on the window ledge and fingered the fringe of light brown hair at the back of his balding head as he drove toward Osteria Cantoro, windows down on this hot midweek morning. He never celebrated birthdays, never even knew his real date. He was born in that horrible apartment his mother hung out in. She'd varied the date over the years, but after she died and he was baptized, he'd claimed the birth year of 1973. He kept this secret from everyone except the Cardinal, but his half century mark was coming to punish him next week. And now he had that other secret to keep.

Years had flown by faster than the cypress trees he sped past on the road. His cheeks flared with shame and sorrow. He pictured what had greeted him on his thirteenth birthday—his mother's mini-skirted body lying in the gutter. Thank God for Father Joseph taking him in. Back in the days when Wild Vines Abbey still housed orphans.

Vito had invited the young men from Wild Vines to meet with Dei Patris today, to add the force of youthful energy.

Working together, Dei Patris and the young men could construct a plan. Tommaso scowled. Carlo had reported seeing Mary and others meeting in Giulia's back room. Women were rising like swells in a tidal wave.

He squeezed his Fiat 500 into a spot on the street not far from Osteria Cantoro and hurried into the bustling restaurant. There was the whole Cantoro family, all ages working together. His heart was touched at the sight of the eight-year-old twins. Tommaso would have had brothers and sisters, too, if his mother hadn't murdered them. Abortion. There could be no greater sin.

He savored the aroma of today's sizzling Bistecca but hurried through the back passage and down to the cellar, ready to set the tone. He was Father Tommaso. Fathers must show the way, even if only by the pale and flickering light of candles on the wall.

He took the chair to the right of Roger, already seated at the head of the long table, set as usual with Chianti, bruschetta and small bowls of strawberries.

Roger scowled. "Vito's bringing the young men. He alerted me they've been wounded by the way women are so choosy. They're coming from anger and need healing."

"The wounded can be the healers," said Tommaso.

Roger nodded and tapped a small gold pin on his lapel. "Did you know Mussolini called for Italian women to have a dozen children each?" As Roger removed his finger from the pin, Tommaso could see the shape of a baby's footprint.

The Cardinal joined them at the table, wearing his red sash, a book clutched under his arm. "We are blessed with our new Prime Minister." He slapped his chest. "She says, 'I'm Georgia, I'm a woman, I'm a mother, I'm a Christian'!"

"Ah, Georgia Meloni." Professor Frank took the last steps two at a time and hung his backpack over the back of a chair. "On the record as against abortion. Italians have sent a clear message."

"Yet still, we are backsliding," Tommaso said. He turned his attention to the stairway where Vito was descending. Two young men followed, dressed in white shirts and khaki shorts. One was tall, well-muscled, and clean-shaven with a mop of blond hair. He carried himself with a lifted chin.

A few steps behind came a slight fellow, head bent, looking down at the steps. Last to step onto the packed earth floor, the young man raised his head, his olive-skinned face pinched into a grimace over his scruffy chin-strap beard.

Vito turned to pat the first young man on the back. "Meet Albert, an American expat."

Roger nodded. "Expat, like me. Have a seat."

"And this is Xavier, a native son." Vito ruffled the sleeve of the slight young man, who nodded in acknowledgment. "He was raised at the Abbey and knows the place inside and out."

Vito pulled out a chair for Xavier. Albert walked to the other side and took a place across from them.

Vito studied each man at the table as if measuring their alignment before he spoke. "Yesterday, I found my way up the hillside from Voce Sotto, and Xavier showed me around. Abbazia dell'uva Selvatica is a secluded place. We can make fine wine from wild grapes there, so to speak." Vito smiled.

Roger's lips puckered. "We know the foundation of the problem is that countries will dwindle to nothing if we cannot stop women from killing babies. In the US, Rush Limbaugh—God Rest His Soul—warned us about 'Feminazis,' telling us the most important thing in the world was seeing that as many abortions as possible take place." Roger rubbed his baby footprint pin with his fingertips. "Did you know Mussolini outlawed abortion? Said it was a crime against humanity." He brought the pin to his lips for a kiss. "What can we do to halt the massacre?"

Tommaso looked around the table at the solemn faces. Young Xavier cleared his throat and pointed at the book the Cardinal had set down on the table. Its cover showed men in top hats poking at flames licking the legs of three women. In a soft voice, Xavier said, "I was taught that midwives kill children and offer them to the devil. The *Malleus* says the only certain way to end the evils of witchcraft is to use torture to get confessions."

Pietro had just come down from cooking at the grill, and he said, "Torture? I'm against any kind of torture. What do you mean? What is the *Malleus*?"

The Cardinal held up the book. "It was written long ago and means the Hammer of Witches," he said. "It was to help find women causing anguish and return them to blessed lives." His voice was clear, soft and tender, almost mesmerizing, thought Tommaso.

"How do you know of the *Malleus*, son?" The Cardinal smiled at Xavier.

Xavier wiped his forehead with the sleeve of his white shirt. "Father Joseph would hurry me away from the village square, where women haggled with butchers on market day. He took me to the bookshop and set me on a stool to look through the witches' book, warned me to stay away from women."

The Cardinal tapped on the book cover and said, "Go on, son."

"I studied the book for years," Xavier said. "It could be of great assistance in understanding the problem, Sir, although I dream of kinder methods to solve it."

Vito stood. "My HypnoConvert method has persuaded women away from going to get their babies killed," said Vito. "No need for some kind of outdated burning at the stake."

"I should hope not! Outrageous!" shouted Pietro.

The Cardinal stood, his face aglow, his red sash

straining over his puffed-up chest. "Torture is only used when necessary, Pietro, and rarely did burning at the stake take place and only as a merciful way to keep the soul pure." He held up the book. "Continually in print, this guide is for hunting witches, but we have no need to hunt because now abortionists operate right out in the open."

Pietro gasped. "Don't you understand that the stereotype of witch burning in the Middle Ages was not accurate? It was just to discredit Catholics by the reformers. How can we say we are on the right path if we use extreme tactics? It's love we want to show them."

"It's not extreme," the Cardinal said, "The *Malleus* set out a system that is fair and merciful, even in our time."

Pietro shook his head. "What would the Pope think? Doesn't this kind of drastic action require high ranking men in the church to enact? How can this little group of laymen even consider this tactic, begging your pardon, Cardinal."

"The Pope is too soft, he's bending to the will of the people." The Cardinal waved the book in the air. "Inquisitors of various ranks may arrest or seize a witch, placing her in safe custody, if it seems good to his conscience. Laymen like Albert and Xavier and Vito can start this work in the Wild Vines. Tommaso and I can join them later."

Professor Frank grabbed a fork and waved it in the air. "I propose that when we turn the mind of a midwife away from the slaughter of innocents, we will be on the right track. These women are spiritually lost and need our guidance, our compassion and love, to find the way back to God, our Father."

Pietro and Xavier were frowning and shaking their heads.

Frank pulled a book out of his backpack. "Not just the Hammer, but also Dante, where he spells out the horrors baptized souls will go through if they do not obey God's laws and live…"

Pietro's sister Francesca appeared at the top of the stairs, arms laden with plates. Her helpers followed, and the women stepped down the fan-shaped ventaglio with practiced agility. The men leaned back and made room for the glistening slabs of Bistecca and bowls of white beans to be set before them.

Tommaso's heart swelled at the sight of the women. When they left, he offered a prayer. "Our Father, fuel the flames of desire to lead our families to you. Help us follow you in our daily lives as imitatores Dei Patris. Bless this food as strength for our mission. We ask this in the name of your son Jesus, and in the power of the Holy Spirit. Amen."

With a grin, Carlo forked into his Bistecca, concentrating on the fragrant and substantial meal. Tommaso joined in with the men, who ate in a monastic stillness, washing down the rich food with light and acidic Chianti Classico. As a digestif after the meal, some poured aged grappa neat into shot glasses. Tommaso hoped they could carry on with focus on the issue at hand and was glad to see Albert and Xavier decline the sixty-proof grappa.

"Siamo alla frutta." Roger shoved back his chair, the wooden legs screeching on the stone floor. He stood and reached over to pluck a ripe strawberry from the bowl. "We are at the fruit, the end of the meal. We may be at the end of more than our meal today, my brothers. I've heard leftists call Italy 'a Country for Old Men' and it will become that if the demonic baby killing is not stopped."

"Women have all the advantages now. The world isn't fair to men," said Albert. He yanked a strawberry from the bowl in front of him. He chomped it in half, then ate the rest, stem and all, washing it down with the last of his Chianti.

Roger nodded. "The extreme crisis of our time calls for extreme measures. Which woman will best serve as an example of how to return to the will of our Father?"

Tommaso's heart thumped hard in his chest. Who would be offered up? Should he suggest someone?

Frank held up his copy of Dante's *Inferno*. "Our first soul to save should be an influencer. I propose a newly certified midwife who claims she is a healer, a member of the leftist party and a supporter of Ellie Schlein."

He pulled a black and white photo from between the pages of the *Inferno* and waved it back and forth. "Trota Mancini. She is baptized Catholic and claims to be straight, but she passionately supports the

LGBT community and the so-called right to choose. She works as a midwife in Rome, publicly pronouncing a need to help the poor get the health care they deserve. Translation—abortion."

Hearing about the poor in Rome reminded Tommaso of his mother. He ran his finger between his collar and his neck, wiping the sweat away. "Prostitutes call themselves sex workers now instead of the sinners they are." He stared at Frank. "Women like this Trota terminate the pregnancies of prostitutes and decent married women both, and call it health care. It's murder!"

Frank raised his eyebrows. "Yes, and she is slated to speak at the Pride parade, along with Rome's mayor, on behalf of their so-called progressive agenda touting their latest crimes against nature."

"What does she look like?" asked Xavier.

Frank passed the photo over to Xavier. "She has glossy black hair, stands 5' 6" and weighs barely a hundred pounds." He slithered his hand down his cheek and along his chest down to his thigh. "She's snello, slim as a virgin."

Tommaso wondered about the grin on Albert's face as the young man heard the word virgin.

Frank carried on. "When I met Trota on campus, she was in a graduating class of midwives. I thought she was the kind I wanted for a wife, fit and pure, but after one date, she never gave me another chance. And I saw her yesterday, passing these out in front of our main building."

He held up a flyer showing a fist clutching a Euro and the wording "You deserve equal health care!" At the bottom was the political party's website. "She was pulling them from her carryall and practically forcing them into students' hands. I tried to get her to go have coffee, but she refused."

The Cardinal stood and held his hand over the red sash crossing his chest. "You realize, friends, that we not only witness the sin of murder of the unborn, but we are dealing with heretics!" He looked around the table. Tommaso pursed his lips and frowned.

The Cardinal read from a page in the *Malleus.* "'A heretic initiates or follows new and false opinions'." He looked up. "It is a form of infidelity, in that a woman believes something in her inner thoughts which is contrary to the true faith."

Pietro protested loudly. "Just a minute! How can we know someone's inner thoughts?"

"We can only judge the inner as it is reflected by actions, and this Trota's actions are clear. She's promoting the devil's work and luring others to sin." The Cardinal slammed closed the book.

Xavier shook his head and murmured, "She has abandoned the church, left it for dead."

Frank chimed in, "According to St. Jerome, the meaning of heresy is choice. God gave us free will and the power of choice. Spreading ideas against the church's pro-life orthodoxy is heresy, a crime. It is choosing evil."

"Trota shows she has no respect for church

doctrine, so let us proceed to gently relocate her, and let us engage Vito," the Cardinal took a breath and nodded at Vito, "to practice his approach to exorcising demons."

Albert said, "I know my way around Rome. Xavier and I can find this woman at the place of the Pride speeches and take her to the Abbey."

Pietro stood. "You realize this is high crime and morally unjust? I can't have you plotting kidnap here in my cellar like Mafia, without objecting."

The others sat solemnly in a moment of silence. No one responded.

"We will be very gentle. Not to hurt her, but to save her," said Vito. "I have had the best training in the HypnoConversion method, I assure you, and teach it now, myself."

Carlo broke the quiet, saying, "I can help move her." No one responded to Carlo.

"Thank you, Albert, for offering your car. The speeches will be at the Tazza Cafe, near the parade route," said Frank. "The mayor will be speaking for his party's stand to support surrogacy." Frank shuddered.

Albert nodded. "During his speech, to distract while we lead Trota to come with us, we can set off some explosives."

"Bombs? Bombs can hurt innocent bystanders," protested Pietro.

"Just small ones, very small, noisy but no shrapnel, like firecrackers."

Tommaso rocked gently in his chair, satisfied with the day's meeting. It wasn't necessary for him to bring up any names.

He reflected on the shape Dei Patris was taking. The two expat Americans, Roger and Albert, strengthened the core group of native Italians, the Cardinal and Frank.

Tommaso was worried about loose-lipped and careless Carlo and peaceful Pietro. But, he had faith in Vito, the learned and experienced man for the job, now holding a shot glass high in the air, with grappa quivering at the rim.

"Dio Santo!" Chords stood out on Vito's neck. "Dio Santo! Let us go forward to save the women from their sins. Return my Joleen to me." He downed his grappa in one swallow.

Tommaso wondered which of the men would be the most effective. Only time would tell. But he didn't have much time left.

8
SISTER FREDERICKA

Fredericka gazed at the green pastures and olive groves as the autobus made its way through the countryside northeast of Rome. At a turn in the road, the window became a mirror, and she tucked a flyaway strand of red hair into the black and blue print scarf she'd tied at the nape of her neck. Their order no longer required them wearing a habit or forced them to travel in pairs as if they couldn't be trusted.

At the stop two blocks past Valdos Verde's parish church, Fredericka got off the air-conditioned bus and strode into the cafe. Adjusting herself to the heat in the room, she inhaled the fragrance of the cafe's signature pizza capriccios—topped with ham, mushrooms, and olives. Giulia herself turned away from the blazing brick oven and waltzed over to greet Fredericka with a kiss on each cheek. "Welcome!" In a lower tone, she added, "Mother Catherine phoned and said you would be joining the women in the back room today."

Giulia dipped her chin in the direction of a man sitting at a table on which was a large untouched pizza. Fiddling with his phone, he looked at Giulia every few seconds. She murmured, "Ignore him, that's Carlo, my brother." She nodded toward a door in the far corner of the room. "Over there. No need to knock, just go in. They're expecting you."

Once inside the back room, Fredericka was pleased to see Mary Tofana seated at a long table. Fredericka had worked with Mary a few weeks ago, with preliminary plans for this march. A stack of white poster boards was at one end of the table and a couple tambourines and reed pipes sat at the other end.

"Welcome, Sister." Mary stood to hug Fredericka. "Meet my college friend, Delilah, here from California. I took her to Mass Sunday, so she's familiar with our dear Father Tommaso and his views."

Fredericka laughed and reached out a hand to the blonde newcomer, who stopped writing on a poster board to shake hands.

Three other women entered the room, the last shutting the door quietly. They burst out laughing. "Not supposed to let on what we're doing in here," said another in a stage whisper.

They hugged Mary and introduced themselves to Delilah and Fredericka.

"Okay, ladies," Mary said. "We don't have much

time before Sister Fredericka has to get back to Rome. She's here to give us details on the story of Marina the Monk, to give us ideas for our signs. After she leaves, we can finish them."

One of the newcomers asked how they would be getting to the march.

"Rosetta has offered to transport us in her van," said Mary. "She'll drop us off at the foot of the bridge across from Castel Sant'Angelo. From there we can walk across the bridge and then turn to march down the Via della Conciliazione, ending at St. Peter's Square."

"But we won't get press coverage with just the few of us here," said Rosetta, wrinkling her nose.

Mary smiled. "I've got assurances from twenty or so WOW members, to join us for the walk."

The woman next to Rosetta frowned. "WOW?"

"Women's Ordination Worldwide," answered Mary. "They started working towards allowing women to be deacons and priests in the Catholic Church a quarter century ago. Twenty-five years! The movement is growing stronger each year, but the opposition is, too. We should expect Vatican security will keep their eyes on us, and pray that is more of a blessing than a curse."

She crossed herself. "And now, let's hear from Sister Fredericka." Mary pulled out a chair and sat.

Fredericka said a silent prayer, opened her backpack and took out the drawings she'd sketched on scrap paper. She pointed to rays of light shining from

Saint Marina's face—rays in pink, blue and white. "I adapted this icon from one I found on the internet."

She passed the drawing to Mary to hand around to the others. "June 18 is the official church feast day for Saint Marina the M—"

Someone was knocking at the door. Fredericka raised her eyebrows and looked at Mary, who got up. She went to the door and opened it a crack. The aroma of pizza tickled Frederick's nostrils again.

A booming voice filled the room. "Looking for the toilette degli uomini."

"The toilet is in the other corner, as you well know," Mary said, closing the door. She turned to the group. "That's Carlo. He's been shadowing me. Seems on the Mafioso side. I think Father Tommaso sent him to spy on us."

Fredericka took a deep breath. "Father Tommaso. Just try to ignore him, stay calm. Marina had to hide her whole life. "

The five women nodded solemnly as Fredericka began again. "Marina was born in 5th century Lebanon. While she was young, her mother died, and she was raised by her father. When she was grown, her father told her he was leaving her an inheritance because he was called by God to enter a monastery. Marina insisted she had the same calling and begged her father to take her with him, to save her soul. He was shocked, but when she told him she would cut her hair and dress in men's clothing, he agreed to her plan."

"Women couldn't be monks, of course," said Mary with a scowl. "Then, or now."

Fredericka held up a drawing of two figures, one bearded and one smooth faced, at the front door of the entrance to a monastery. "She and her father changed her name to Marinos, and they joined the monastic community together."

"Wow," said Rosetta. She took a poster board from the stack and began drawing her own version of Marina's face.

"Yes, wow," Fredericka continued. "The newly named Marinos excelled in spiritual practice. Dressed as a man, she fasted regularly and had the gift of healing through the laying on of hands. She was addressed by her fellow monastics as 'Abba Marinos' meaning Father Marinos. On one occasion, the Abbot himself went to Marinos and asked him to travel with three other brothers to attend to business affairs of the community. This took them some distance and required an overnight stay at an inn."

"Bet they didn't have food there as good as Giulia's," sang out Delilah. "She's sending in pizza for us later."

Fredericka's stomach growled, and she laughed. "Pretty sure you're right. Anyway, that innkeeper had an unmarried daughter, who after the monks' stay, began to put on weight, and it was not from overeating that good food. She was pregnant."

"OMG," whispered Rosetta.

"When asked who fathered the unborn child, the

innkeeper's daughter blamed Marinos. The innkeeper traveled to the monastery and reported the accusation to the Abbot. When confronted, Marinos offered no defense, only acknowledging herself to be sinful before the Lord.

"Seeing no other recourse, the Abbot expelled Marinos from the monastery. Marinos remained outside the gate, living in abject penitence. When the innkeeper later brought his daughter's newborn son to Marinos, the infant was adopted and raised by Marinos, fed by milk donated from nearby shepherds."

Fredericka paused and looked at the faces before her, each bearing her own unique expression of sorrow.

"Eventually, the monks convinced the Abbot to let Marinos rejoin them, as long as he did 'hard labor' such as cooking, cleaning, and childcare, in addition to other duties. Marinos raised the boy to adulthood, with him believing all the while that Marinos was his father. Following in his 'father's' footsteps, he himself went on to join the same monastery."

Rosetta's jaw hung slack, her marker set aside on the poster board. "Da non crederce," she whispered. "Unbelievable."

Fredericka nodded. "One morning, when Marinos did not arrive for community services, the brothers discovered his dead body in his monastic cell. Upon preparing Marinos' body for burial, the brothers discovered that Marinos had been born female. Upon this revelation, the Abbot fell down beside Marinos' body, weeping and saying: 'I will remain here at his holy feet until I die, if I do not receive forgiveness.' In response, the voice of Marinos was then heard forgiving him. Upon learning of Marinos' birth as a female, the innkeeper's daughter confessed to her false accusation, and spent the rest of her life in penitence at the tomb of Marinos. All the surrounding community then came to know that Marinos was a saint, and was the woman named Marina, who gave up her life as a woman, to save her soul."

Tears brimming at the edge of her brown eyes, Rosetta shook her head. "Just what my sisters would have to do to follow their call to ordination. Become a man."

Sister Fredericka nodded slowly. She held up another drawing of Marina. "Instead of marching on June 18, her official church feast day, we are marching on June 17, a Saturday, when we hope more people are out to witness. Let's get some terrific posters made to honor Marina the Monk."

"We are planning to sing as we cross the Tiber," said Mary. "It helps get press coverage." She picked up a tambourine. "Nothing so American as this song, of course." She kept time with the tambourine as she sang "Shall We Gather at the River," and Delilah harmonized.

Fredericka smiled at their enthusiasm. The reality might not turn out to be so much fun.

9
HILLARY

Hillary's eyes roamed Southside Park, searching for anything out of the ordinary. Arcs of red, blue and yellow balloons floated over the exuberant crowd. Ed had reminded her it was a challenge to spot a crime about to happen, unless you saw a person leaving a package or backpack and walking away. Or coming at you with a weapon. Hillary had foiled a few crimes in the past, but none during a parade.

Dressed in her new Love is Love tee shirt, Claire was waving a Pride flag, hopping from one foot to another and chatting with her friends, all of them antsy for the parade to get moving.

Fear nibbled at Hillary. These girls thought they were street smart, going to be seniors in high school in the fall. But they hadn't faced any real dangers yet. Were any homophobes lurking among the marchers? How could anyone tell? Thank God, Claire still wore the St. Goretti medal Hillary'd given her for protection, even though she kept it inside her shirts.

Uniformed city police stood alert and smiling at the marchers. Local TV crews had their equipment set up. Hillary surveyed the crowd, her muscles tense, at the ready. Years ago, her sensei had trained her to watch the eyes of opponents. The eyes often forecast what people were planning to do. Like that time Hillary's cousin was about to serve poisoned coffee at a wedding reception. But this huge parade was so different.

Hillary searched faces nearby, looking for anything suspicious. She prayed they would be spared any violence, like when a gunman killed a teenager at a Mardi Gras celebration this spring in New Orleans.

AT LAST, THE THRONG STARTED MOVING ALONG 9TH Street toward Capitol Mall. Claire and her friends rushed forward. Hillary struggled to push her way through the crowd as if swimming through people, but she soon lost track of Claire.

This is not abandoning your daughter, she told herself. She worked her way to the sidewalk and marched along, looking side to side, ninety degrees, back and forth, for any hint of danger, listening for gunshots between the singsong chanting of "Out of the Closets and into the Streets!"

As she passed a state government building, Hillary

glimpsed movement at a second-floor window. It was just someone inside jiggling a small rainbow flag.

Ahead, screaming broke out over the sing-song chanting. The flow of marchers slowed.

"Bombs!"

"Watch out!"

Hillary darted ahead on the sidewalk and reached the place where Claire lay fallen to the ground. Hillary stumbled and fell to the street, landing a few feet from Claire.

Rivulets of red ran down Claire's face. Marchers moved on around them, laughing. Claire was nearly being buried in the crowd. Screams turned into shrieks.

Laughing, Claire's friends pulled her up at the same time they helped Hillary stand. One friend's face was splattered with blue, and another's was washed in bright yellow.

Claire and her friends pulled up the bottoms of their tee shirts and mopped at their cheeks and hair. They pointed to an old Victorian. People on the balcony were heaving water balloons at the marchers and shouting "Here's gold at the end of the rainbow!"

Hillary was stunned. A water balloon shower.

A police officer with a bullhorn ordered those on the balcony to quit throwing the balloons. "Stop! That is assault. It is a crime!"

Someone was screaming, "Kill the gays!"

Hillary couldn't tell where the screams were

coming from. Claire and her friends moved forward again.

Darting glances through the crowd, Hillary kept pace alongside the marchers. From across the street, a short figure in a plain black tee and nondescript shorts rushed through the crowd. He waved a knife in Claire's direction. "Abomination!" he yelled.

Hillary thrust her hand out past the knife and grabbed his wrist. In one motion, she twisted his arm behind his back and lifted him off his feet, the knife still clutched in his fist.

"We've got him," shouted a city cop. Hillary let go, as the little man shrieked, "Abom, abom, abom!" Two officers whisked him over to the sidewalk and down an alley to a waiting patrol car.

Adrenaline fueled for whatever else might lay in wait as the parade snaked its way toward the capitol, Hillary caught up with Claire.

10
HILLARY

Home from the parade, Hillary retraced her steps along the pathway to Paisley's cottage and knocked on the door. She counted to ten and knocked again.

Paisley opened the door, frowning. "Yes?"

Hillary pushed in past her mother and stamped her foot on the floor. "Claire nearly got knifed today. What would it have cost you to be with us? Just a few hours." She swept her arm toward the easel. "That sunrise could have waited, yes?"

"It's a sunset," Paisley said. "Part of the series I'm shipping to Italy."

"Oh, well, you can't stop painting for a second, can you? What about the hours I spent rescuing you from that man?"

"That was different. You're overreacting. Claire is smart and capable. She is fine, or you wouldn't be here haranguing me."

"She's barely fine! If you'd been with us, you could have shouted a warning about the man with the knife. Aren't you even a little bit sorry?"

Paisley held her brush in the air and waved it as if conducting an orchestra. "I love Claire, but I'm not sorry."

"Why can't you say you're sorry? For not being with us today? Let alone for leaving when I was ten! Would that be so hard?" Hillary's pulse raced.

Paisley leaned closer to Hillary. "Don't be childish." She stabbed the canvas with red paint. "I left you in your father's good hands."

"How did you know he wouldn't spend all his time at the newspaper writing his stories and ignore me?"

"I could tell."

"How?"

Paisley dropped her paint brush into a ceramic jar and swept her white hair off her forehead. "The way he cuddled you when he was home. The way he wouldn't let me take you from him, lying on his chest while he rubbed your back. He loved soothing you."

Hillary's face grew hot. It was true. Her father had taken her with him everywhere after her mother left, had raised her to be a reporter herself. Now he was twenty years dead, in newspaper heaven or hell.

Unwilling to credit the truth, Hillary stared wordless at Paisley, who kept talking. "As you grew, he loved how neat you were, just like him, the perfect newsman, writing clean copy first draft. I knew you would be all right." She took a clean brush and used it to lift blue-gray paint off her palate, swishing it in leaden streaks across the top third of her canvas.

Hillary flashed on her father's proud face as he would toss the newspaper on the coffee table and her own joy in writing articles. Until she had those panic attacks when assigned to cover a story about mothers. "But I hated not having a mother."

Paisley glared at her and shouted, "We all hate lots of things. I hated being ignored. I took up art, sat at the feet of my teacher, and …" she lowered her voice, "got pregnant. Your father would have kicked me out, knowing it was not by him, so I ran off with Bill when he got the job in Tahiti."

Hillary had heard that before but hearing it now carried her into an altered state. She whispered, "What happened to that baby?"

Paisley set her brush down and went to the window. She looked out at a white peony bush. Hillary could see ants crawling all over the petals.

"Billy died when he was two, a car accident, with Bill at the wheel, fueled on vodka. He stopped painting and lost his job. I tried to sell my work, but I hadn't developed yet." She waved her hands as if flying. "We had to move and live with his sister in Kona. The vodka swamped Bill, and he stumbled around town, brought home dangerous people. I needed protection."

She pulled out a cord from inside her smock. "A Hawaiian friend made me this necklace." She twirled two carved beads strung onto the cord. "They are handles, if you use the twisted coconut husk as a strangling cord."

Hillary felt the blood drain from her face. Her mother could really help in a dangerous situation. "A strangling cord?"

Paisley shook her head. "I never needed it. Bill was later killed when he walked out in front of a bus in downtown Kona. A tourist bus, would you believe!"

Paisley stuck the cord back inside her smock and returned to her easel. She moved the sunset painting to the floor.

She squeezed a glob of red paint out of a tube and added it to her pallet. "Am I really what you accused me of? A narcissist. What colors would that take?" She scraped a knife against the thin wooden edge of her pallet, drawing it all the way down and off. She wiped the knife against a damp rag hanging from the easel.

Hillary watched, wordless and enthralled.

"What color for a narcissist? Red? Bold. Loud. Attention getting. 'Look at me, look at me.' The way Jake would crow when he came home with another headline story. Show it off to me, trapped at home with a screaming baby. Jake would throw the newspaper on the blue and white tile coffee table and point to his byline printed there above the fold."

Hillary could visualize the scene.

"What colors for a bunch of loud shouting newsmen?" Paisley asked. "Black and white and red all over like the old newspaper joke? Yes, white. All of them white men back in the day when paper conveyed the news."

Hillary nodded, recalling those days back when she was still a reporter.

"I was so intimidated," Paisley said. "I had to run away to become who I am, run away from him and his shadow." She squeezed white onto the pallet, then a blazing red. Her breath quickened. "I left you in order to care for my survival. Does that really make me a narcissist?"

Paisley turned away and hauled a blank canvas onto the easel.

Hillary resisted the urge to kick the canvas to the floor. She let herself out of the cottage, swallowing her own fiery words. Who was this woman? What did Hillary want from her? Need from her? Hillary could never forgive her even if she ever humbled herself to apologize.

11
XAVIER

Xavier placed the egg cartons into a wire box in the trunk. With his fingertips on the trunk lid, he gave it a light push, listening for the latch to close. He yanked open the passenger door, whirled his backpack onto the floor, and slid onto the leather seat. "Let's get on the road."

Albert revved the 3.6 Pentastar V6 engine and backed his black Lancia Thema out from the courtyard. He cruised at eight kph down the village street, keeping the engine noise to a low hum.

Good, thought Xavier, no speeding this cool morning. Nothing to spark the Polizia to pull them over. Nothing for breakfast either. His stomach was empty, the way he liked it, so all his energy could go to his brain. Today, he would need his wits about him.

Xavier made the sign of the cross over himself at the thought of a police checkpoint. It could happen. The Pride parade in Rome was the kind of event that might call for one. They could be set up anywhere, anytime, without warning and were sometimes manned by submachine-gun-toting cops sporting bullet proof vests. He hoped packing the explosives in an egg carton would be convincing if they were stopped. They would say they were on their way to deliver fresh eggs from Señora Bozzano in the village. Dressed in white Chambray summer suits, they looked so fresh themselves, innocent, eager and excited, they would surely not be halted more than a few minutes on the way to Rome.

Getting back to the village and up to the abbey later with their captive might be a different matter. Xavier reviewed the checklist in his mind, no need to put their plans to paper. "Let's go over the time-frame." He enumerated the steps of their plan and listened for Albert's corrections. There were none.

Albert slowed to let Xavier out of the Lancia before he edged the car inches away from the four-story building on the Via di Sant'Agata de Goti, far away enough from the Coliseum where there was still some parking. A man in a rumpled gray hoodie sat on the stoop of a dress shop a few doors down, shoving spaghetti from a paper plate into his mouth with his fingers, not giving them a second look.

Albert got out, opened the rear door, and retrieved their suit jackets off the hangers. They put on their jackets, and Albert popped open the trunk.

Xavier reached in and opened the blanket holding three egg cartons, stacked one on top of the other. They'd figured any checkpoint cops would not search the top carton but go down to the second or third one, so they'd packed the explosives on top.

He lifted the egg carton lid and looked at the dozen little bombs that would create a distraction. With everyone's attention on the explosions, people would never see what the two of them were really there for.

One at a time, he gingerly handed six little bombs, each the size of a small egg, to Albert and watched him lower them down into his trouser pockets. Albert smirked and thrust his pelvis forward to accentuate the bulge of the bombs. "The long jacket barely hides my three packages," Albert said, leering at his friend.

Xavier nodded. "Un figo. What a Chad you look today," he said and looped a lanyard holding Albert's press pass over his friend's head.

Albert let out the bark he used for a laugh. "Members of the press. The stories I could tell, you couldn't stomach." He grabbed his Leica M10. Xavier took the empty egg carton and scooped up the other two, full of eggs. He set them down beside the man eating spaghetti. "Get these to somebody's kitchen to cook them for you. Buon appetito."

Xavier led the way down the narrow street to the neighborhood square, packed with revelers, their painted faces grinning and arms reaching out for group hugs while dancing about half naked on the dark sampietrini cobblestones. Albert was already engaged in snapping photos.

Xavier maneuvered himself to keep the living palate of body paints from rubbing up against his white suit while at the same time, smiling and nodding to match the festivities. But inside, he felt more alone and abandoned than ever, a solitary soul in the buoyant crowd, yearning to belong but afraid of everything around him.

Albert's camera hung down near his press pass as he turned right for the longer walk to the parade route over near the Coliseum, and Xavier followed. They threaded through hundreds of marchers and darted between truck-drawn floats. Rainbows of balloons of all colors bobbed against a blue Italian sky. Shouts of "l'amore e amore" filled the air, smells of pot and oils of all kinds begged to be inhaled. Cacophony reigned, human ecstasy exploded in overlays and kaleidoscopes, in Venn diagrams of Dionysian joy.

As the hot sun approached straight overhead, Xavier pictured the map in his mind and led the way across the buzzing and ebullient boulevard over to the restaurant on a big corner, planters bordering the al fresco tables in front of the restaurant. Amidst the leafy yellow and red blossoms, he tucked his six explosives, spacing them evenly apart. Then he double checked his remote. He nudged Albert. "Plant yours," he mouthed against the roar of the crowd and nodded to a nearby wooden box the size of a coffin, bordering several wrought iron tables, at which people were toasting one another with Aperol Spritzers and munching deep-fried zucchini sticks.

Xavier moved closer to a small space, set up with a mic. He looked toward the restaurant's building. The pair of politicians leading Italy's progressive party should be here by now. He walked closer to the man at the podium who asked in a hoarse whisper if he would like to be seated.

Xavier waved his press pass. "Here for the speeches."

The man nodded. "They've been delayed in the parade."

Xavier hadn't wanted to be noticed. He nodded and paced the al fresco dining platform perimeter, noting again their exit street and keeping an eye on the mic. Albert seemed to have disappeared. Suddenly, the crowd chatter faded as people started clapping. Some pumped their fists in the air. There were Democratic Party leaders near the mic, with Rome's Mayor Gualtieri at their side. He bent near the mic and said, "Welcome to the party! Our progressive party!"

The crowd chanted, "Gay and here to stay!"

The mayor waited a few beats before he carried on. "As you know, earlier this year, the government headed by far-right Premier Giorgia Meloni told municipal officials when recording births, to register only the biological parent, and not the other parent in a same-sex couple." The crowd booed long and loud before it quieted down for the mayor to continue.

"Today, we are announcing our party's campaign to certify both parents on every birth certificate, no cancellations!" The mayor said, "Yesterday, I defied Meloni's order. I registered with emotion and conviction, the birth certificates of children born to same-sex couples."

The crowd cheered at every pause in the mayor's speech confirming the party's support of gay parents to full legal status. He introduced the party leaders and Trota Mancini, as chair of the Human Health Rights wing of the party.

So, thought Xavier, there she was. A young woman with shiny black hair, so slender she almost looked like she suffered from some chronic illness. Easy pickings, like Professor Frank said. Trota Mancini. Right next to the mayor, who concluded his remarks with, "Go, rejoin the parade, and celebrate with Pride."

As people seated at tables gathered their things, Xavier pressed the button on his remote.

12
HILLARY

Hillary and Claire walked through the courtyard and into Trinity Cathedral's Great Hall for the Pride Youth Sunday festival. Banners of all colors hung from the ceiling, emblazoned with names and symbols of the Northern California diocese's parish churches. Booths lined the walls, their counters stacked with pamphlets explaining what each group was doing to support young people in the region.

The *Sacramento LGBT Community Center* was highlighting their advocacy for equity & justice. Hillary talked to a fresh-faced young man seated in the booth. "I'd love a speaker for the Intro to Ethnic Studies class I teach," she said.

"Sure!" He ruffled the quiff of purple hair at the top of his head. "When and where?"

"Not until the fall, and it's down south of town, in Clearwater."

"No problem." He handed her a form. "Just fill this out, and we'll be glad to get you a great presenter." He smiled and patted his chest. "Me!"

Hillary laughed, bent to complete the form, and left it with him.

Claire and one of her friends were at the Red Cross booth. "Yes," said an olive-complected woman wearing a bright red vest. "One of our youth shelters is in Rome and welcomes anyone in need of protection."

"See, Mom," Claire said, "Safety in Rome!"

Hillary put her arm around Claire's waist. "I can still lift you up, anywhere you might be in trouble!" She hoisted her daughter a few inches off the floor and set her down quickly, ducking away from the punches Claire was pulling in her direction.

Leaving her daughter laughing in mock distress with her friend, Hillary headed for the coffee service. Youth shelters. This might be some risky 21st century summer, in ancient Rome.

13
XAVIER

Xavier waited for Albert to move near the mayor as if to protect him, as the bombs began exploding. Slices of oranges and lemons flew through the air. Cocktail glasses collided in flight and smashed into shards.

Young and old screamed and ran, turning over tables that crashed to the cobblestones. Flowers, leaves and dirt shot high into the sky as the blasts boomed louder than noises from the parade. The smell of gunpowder permeated the air.

Xavier pulled Trota away from the chaos and slid his arm around her waist as if rescuing her. "What?" she shouted, her dark eyes bulging.

He nodded at his press pass. "Let's move you to safety."

"Get my carryall!"

He quick-stepped her away from the throng.

"My carryall!" she yelled.

He pulled his white handkerchief from his coat pocket, and clamped it over her face, breaking the capsule and releasing the fumes. Her slender body sagged against his. There was Albert at her other side, lifting her arm to put it around his waist. They hustled her to a side street as others dashed away, fleeing the site of the explosions.

"Too much celebration," Albert explained to an onlooker as they whisked Trota's limp body along between them. "Getting her to the cafe for coffee."

Once past the neighborhood plaza and back on the Via di Sant'Agata de Goti, they laid her inert body in the trunk, bent her legs to follow the shape of the wire box now empty of the three egg cartons. Xavier slammed the lid shut, grateful that the man in the gray poncho was asleep on the dress shop steps, his paper plate fallen to the cobblestone street, the egg cartons stacked next to the wall. No witnesses.

Albert jumped into the driver's seat and fired up the Lancia. He pulled away from the building and stopped to let Xavier in. We got away with it, thought Xavier. Now go home, take a sinner with us for her salvation.

14
SISTER FREDERICKA

Fredericka stood in the shade of the covered walkway and watched Pauline, who'd tucked her summer-weight habit into the crease between her thighs and calves and was crab walking between two rows of tomatoes. Fredericka had to smother a laugh.

What a strong spirit Sister Pauline was. With her blue veil pinned back, she'd rolled up her sleeves and held them clenched against her sides. Slim and sinewy, she was known for helping guests with issues to talk over.

Weeding necessitated rubbing up against the plants, but the powder on the stems made Fredericka itch like crazy, so she seldom worked in the garden. She was busy with the guest house laundry and traveling to help Mary and the other women up in Valdos Verde village plan their strategies.

Pauline tossed the weeds into a cart she pushed along ahead of her. Watching her was like a meditation, and Fredericka's mind drifted in the warm Italian afternoon. Fredericka had laid her mother in the grave last year. With her last words, her mother encouraged her to cleanse ancient poisons from the church. Fredericka closed her eyes and measured the miracle of her breath, her time here and now, part of the gathering force from the ancient body, the original female body, broken for others to be born.

"Hello," sang out Sister Pauline, startling Fredericka, who jerked back to the reality of the day. "What brings you out here? I thought it was your day for laundry?"

"Anna's doing it instead," Fredericka said. "I've been ordered to go see Father Tommaso."

"Ordered?"

Mother Catherine stepped out into the garden sunlight. "Father Tommaso phoned me to say he saw Sister Fredericka on TV, circling the Triton Fountain along with protestors demanding to see the topic of women's ordination added to the papal calendar."

Fredericka appreciated how Mother Catherine kept tabs on the whole body of Christ, the male and the female, all of them. She knew when to keep and when to reveal a secret.

"He keeps his finger on the pulse of the public, he does," said Fredericka.

"Yes, he reminded me of his belief that malevolent forces are battling for control of our land. He told me he was not pleased to see a nun from my convent out in public like that."

"Why does he care about us down here in Rome? He's so far away, up in little Valdos Verde," said Sister Pauline, squinting up against the bright sun.

Mother Catherine said, "A secret I don't tell many is that I grew up in Valdos Verde, myself. I reached out to Tommaso, phoned him when I was appointed the superior here, became Mother Catherine. Pray he doesn't start asking about what any of the rest of us might be up to. You know the rumor—he looks for wayward sheep to add to his watch list." Mother Catherine bent to pick a ripe cherry tomato, rub it on her long skirt and pop it into her mouth.

Pauline wrinkled her nose in a grimace and moved along the row of tomatoes. "I'm looking for young weeds to pull, along with prickly old ones."

That's what I'm doing, too, Fredericka thought, looking for weeds to pull from God's garden. Weeds like the Vatican policies against letting us serve at all levels.

Fredericka turned and left, unsure how her meeting with Father Tommaso would go. This trip would be so different from the one to Giulia's cafe. Would she be in trouble? It was the uncertainty that made her sick. Just like the Shrove Tuesday Pancake Dinner back in the day. The Parish Hall had been packed with her friends. It should have been such a good time, waiting to hear who won the prize. It was the uncertainty she hated, over who would win the trip to Catholic Kids summer camp. She had won, and that summer had turned her life over to God.

She walked to the bus stop, wondering if she was going to be added to Father Tommaso's watch list. Life was not a lottery, she reminded herself. God was in control. Her job was to listen and hear what the Holy Spirit wanted from her in each moment.

FREDERICKA LISTENED AS FATHER TOMMASO SAID, "There are gateways to darkness that we must all remain watchful of. Protests showing up on TV like that are diabolical." He tapped on his computer monitor. "And then to see it still running on YouTube!" He shook his head. "It's a grave sin, promoting women's ordination even though the Triton does not grab attention as the Trevi does."

"With all respect, Father," she said, "that demonstration was simply asking that the Pope add the topic to the papal calendar. Just discuss the issue."

"What kind of tricky talk is that?" he asked. "What's the difference?"

"An exploration of a subject is never a sin. Think of Isaiah 1:13, 'Come now, let us reason together, says the Lord: though your sins are like scarlet, they shall be as white as snow; though they are red like crimson, they shall become like wool'."

He stared at her, wordless for a moment. "Bless you, Sister. Let me know what other explorations you plan to be involved in."

Fredericka bowed. "Thank you, Father. May the Lord protect us all."

15
FATHER TOMMASO

Tommaso guided his Fiat 500 into a space across the street from Our Lady of the Angels and turned off the engine. Last year, he'd driven here to Flozzia for his confession. The Cardinal had erected a temporary seat in the tiny town, saying its rectory was more comfortable than the one at the cathedral on the far side of the diocese.

Tommaso leaned against the car door for a moment then pushed it open. Using the steering wheel for leverage, he turned, lifted his leg out of the car, and set it onto the packed dirt roadway. With a grunt, he dragged his other leg out and planted both feet on the ground. He took a deep breath before he made a big push to stand up. This must be what the doctor meant. Muscle weakness.

He made it up the gravel pathway to the front door of the old rectory. Before he could lift the brass knocker, the seventy-five-year-old Cardinal came rushing out. "Why didn't you text me? No need for you to have parked." He hurried out to the car, a book in his hand, his briefcase flopping against his leg.

The Cardinal didn't seem to notice Tommaso's struggle to get back into the car. Before Tommaso even fastened his seatbelt, the Cardinal was voicing his excitement. "At last, we are taking action, making an example of repentance. This midwife schemed to destroy the generative force in women by procuring abortion." He patted the worn cover of the *Malleus* on his lap. "She thereby nullifies the force in men as well."

Tommaso's headache was creeping forward from his temples, and it hurt to listen as the Cardinal carried on, nearly shouting. Tommaso and the Cardinal had to witness the midwife's confession. Xavier had texted they better get up to the Abbey right away.

As Tommaso drove through the countryside on the way to the village at the foot of the Abbey, the Cardinal flipped through the pages of the tattered copy of the *Malleus* he held open on his lap. "I pray Trota is ready to confess and repent, now that Vito's worked with her, and she's had time to reflect," he said. "What is it exactly that Vito does in his process?"

Tommaso realized he was not sure of the details. "He pierces through their willful resistance to allow their God-given natures to come forward."

The Cardinal didn't skip a beat in quoting from the *Malleus*, "Witchcraft has been around for centuries, but is emerging once more from the shadows."

WHEN TOMMASO GOT TO VOCE SOTTO, HE struggled to shift his foot from the accelerator to the brake pedal quickly enough so the Cardinal didn't suspect anything. It was getting harder to work the brake and the clutch smoothly together. He wished he'd bought a Fiat 500L instead of his manual transmission 500.

He drove along slowly, looking for the address of Albert's apartment. His fuzzy vision didn't help. He squeezed his eyes nearly shut to bring into focus the numbers on the double doors that guarded each building's entry courtyard.

When he spotted Albert's number painted on a gate in the old, stuccoed wall, Tommaso asked the Cardinal to get out and buzz them into the courtyard. The Cardinal was half again his age yet had more bounce in his step than Tommaso, just turned 50 last week.

After Tommaso got the Fiat 500 parked in the enclosed courtyard, he found getting out of the car easier. The weakness seemed to fade away as the day wore on.

He paid a courtesy call to thank the apartment manager for letting him park next to Albert's Lancia. She was a spry old woman named Eleonora, who repeatedly crossed herself and exclaimed she was honored with the presence of two men of the cloth.

Tommaso headed for the base of the thickly forested hillside. The pathway was familiar to him from decades ago when he'd lived in Father Joseph's orphanage. He'd learned to watch out for the wild pigs rooting for truffles at the base of the oak trees.

Later, he'd moved down to the village. His cheeks warmed at the memory of his wild days, before God the Father called him, and he turned his life around and entered the seminary.

On the overgrown incline, Tommaso had to stop and rest often. He stumbled several times, but did not confess to the Cardinal what was wrong, and instead claimed he wanted to appreciate the view, looking out over the Tuscan countryside below, verdant and bright with sunflowers shooting to the sky on this summer day. As an orphaned teen, he had helped to mend wooden benches placed at intervals up the hillside for visitors who used to trek up to the monastery to buy clay oil lamps and painted crosses. Half the benches had deteriorated but a few stood the test of time and allowed Tommaso to rest a minute.

The Cardinal had walked on ahead and now waited in front of the church with Xavier, as they looked out over the gentle slope of dead grape vines.

Xavier stepped down to greet Tommaso, who took the young man's outreached hand and held it as he stepped up onto the porch, in front of the gap left by the missing wooden doors. Tommaso kissed the young man on both cheeks before he asked, "How is Trota doing? Is she ready to confess?"

Xavier said, "It's gone slower than we hoped." He led Tommaso and the Cardinal into the nave, stopping when the Cardinal halted to gaze at the fresco of the burning women. Tommaso remembered that fresco from the days he lived and worked there with Father Joseph.

The Cardinal nodded with a clenched jaw, then proclaimed, "Fire purifies. Saves souls."

"It's powerful, but there can be other ways," Xavier said in a soft voice, as he led them to the small door at the far left of the altar.

He lit oil lamps for the three of them. "Follow me," he said, and started down the stairs. Tommaso clamped his teeth tight to keep from crying out in pain as he took the stairs slowly down into the dark, damp tunnel.

Xavier halted them at the tomb of Father Joseph. He pointed to the baked clay cover set in over the burial niche and showed them the epitaph he'd incised out of respect for the old priest. Tommaso felt his heart melt at the homage from Xavier to this man who'd served as adopted father to so many abandoned boys.

Xavier led them into an open space. Tommaso had been expecting to find himself in a claustrophobic dungeon. Instead, the clearing was roomy, with space for two bookshelves; and a desk, plus a large worktable and some sort of chair.

Xavier motioned them to set their oil lamps on a shelf. He walked over to the big table and ran both hands over it, fingers splayed out, as if washing it down. "Albert helped me bring this table down in pieces from the old abbey refectory."

The Cardinal nodded. "We came to offer confession and pardon by God's mercy for the offense Trota committed against Him and reconcile her with the Church which she has wounded by her sins. Where is she?"

"I trust you are here in all goodness," said Xavier. On top of the stained walnut planks butted up tightly side by side, he pushed his hands together and formed a cup framing a spot of sunlight shining on the table from an air shaft. "We worked with the midwife all day yesterday, but…"

He turned and waved in the direction of an earthen wall where Tommaso saw Vito sitting by the side of a waist-high niche, a dim tomb space.

"What are you doing?" Tommaso asked.

No one said a word.

Tommaso walked over to the wall. Vito bent over and cupped his head in his hands. Tommaso peered into the niche. A young woman lay inside, motionless.

"What have you done, Vito?" cried Tommaso. "She's still as a corpse."

16
FATHER TOMMASO

Vito looked up at Tommaso with eyes wide as if he'd seen a ghost. Vito shook his head, then he tossed his chin in Albert's direction.

Albert took the cue and said, "When we got back and parked in the courtyard, we went to get her out of the trunk, but she was clutching at her chest and starting to yell she needed her carryall. We couldn't let Eleanora and the renters hear her screaming, so I stuffed a rag in her mouth." He looked at Xavier.

"I pleaded with her," Xavier said. "This is in your best interest. You will thank us later."

Tommaso glared at Albert, who was breathing hard and nodding. He said, "She refused to walk and hung like a dead weight, forcing us to half drag her up the hill. When we carried her down the stairs here, she fought us harder. We had to use more of my aerosol. That put her out. We bundled her in blankets and laid her in the niche. We took turns sitting by her side through the night."

Tommaso couldn't believe his eyes nor his ears. "When were you able to start working with her, Vito?"

"I came yesterday, brought my portable recliner. It cradles the subject, to relax and accept suggestions." He walked over to a corner and lifted an aluminum chair with black webbing straps and spiky aluminum legs, swung it open and set it next to the long table. "You see, rockers can be locked or left to rock freely."

Tommaso said, "I was expecting a typical therapist setting with two comfortable chairs, facing each other. How did you get her into that contraption?"

Vito looked at Albert and Xavier. "The young men carried her gently from the niche and sat her into the recliner."

Tommaso felt weak in the knees. He leaned against the earthen wall to keep from falling. "And…?"

Vito was breathing hard. He looked at Albert. "We kept her lightly sedated." His voice slipped into a dull cadence. "I spoke monotonously to allow her subconscious to be receptive." He shook his head. "After nearly an hour, she still refused to slip into trance. I put a sleep mask on her, satiny and smooth, suggesting the warm quiet of the womb. We played the sound of a mother's heartbeat." He waved his hands in Albert's direction.

Albert poked at his laptop and the room filled with the steady lub-dub of a heart beating.

Tommaso's gut tightened. He swallowed to keep the nausea down. "Go on," he said.

Vito straightened and threw back his shoulders. "As standard practice for tough cases, I massaged around her eyes, gently, at the boney edges."

Tommaso was shocked. "All that touching is normal?"

"Dr. Longosi recommends it for a subject refusing to be put into a trance state. The physical stimulation can subvert the conscious mind and let subconscious desires come to the surface."

Albert scowled. "Desires. Women really just want to serve men." He paused. "That's what's deep in them."

Vito nodded. "People don't want to talk about it, but that is the heroic aspect of womanhood, offering themselves for life to come through. My Joleen is refusing any more babies, rebelling against nature…" His voice caught for a second before he whispered, "And rebellion against God, too. It's heresy."

Tommaso shook his head. "What happen after that?"

"She started screaming for us to get her carryall," said Vito. "I had Xavier run back down to the car to search for anything like that."

"I knew we didn't have it, but I searched the Lancia trunk anyway," said Xavier.

The Cardinal stared speechless at Vito then turned and said to Tommaso, "I trusted you that

Vito's process followed approved protocols and was not some crazy stunt of a practice."

Vito sighed. "I kept track of her pulse, and when her heart was racing and she was gasping for breath, we carried her back to the niche, to let her rest. We piped in lullaby music. She may have fallen into a coma." He was on the verge of tears. "It could be that she is the most suggestible at this time though, truthfully."

The Cardinal moved to the side of the midwife lying in the niche and said, "I will pray." He laid his hand on her arm.

Trota stirred and moaned. She flung his hand away. Her eyes flew open, the whites showing all the way round. "Ni… ni…" she gasped. "Nitro!"

Tommaso stared at Albert. "Did she say anything to you about her heart?"

"Nothing."

The Cardinal reached into his briefcase and pulled out a cross. He waved it alongside Trota in the niche and began praying. "Most glorious Prince of the Heavenly Armies, Saint Michael the Archangel, defend us in our battle against the rulers of this world of darkness, against the spirits of wickedness in the high places who try to inhabit this woman."

Trota whispered, "Ni… Ni…"

The Cardinal prayed, "Padre Nostro, Our Father who art in heaven—"

"What are you doing!" Trota screamed.

Tommaso tugged at the Cardinal's sleeve and

turned him aside. He whispered, "Sinners can be obstinate and freely reject the grace of repentance. They can choose the eternal fires of hell."

The Cardinal shook his head. "There is always hope. Only after death is it too late." He turned back to Trota, and said, "Pray the God of Peace to crush Satan beneath your feet, that he may no longer retain you captive."

"Never," she shouted. "I've never done anything wrong! You are crazy, the bunch of you!"

The Cardinal continued speaking, drowning her out. "We offer our prayers to the Most High, that without delay, the angels may draw His mercy down upon you; take hold of the old serpent, which is the devil and Satan, bind him and cast him into that bottomless pit."

Trota bolted upright. She clawed at the earth above her head and screamed, "My heart!" She stiffened and fell back. "Ni-tro," she whispered.

Vito felt for her pulse. "Move her onto the floor!"

Tommaso stood paralyzed. Xavier and Albert hoisted Trota out of the niche and laid her on the earthen floor.

Vito knelt and did chest compressions, his tears streaming down onto her face. Tommaso watched in horror. The Cardinal was mute. Xavier and Albert paced back and forth from the tunnel to where Trota lay.

At last, Vito stood. "She's gone. Gone straight to hell."

Silence filled the clearing.

Xavier murmured, "Oh my God, she's dead."

"The fucking bitch," said Albert.

Tommaso cried, "How can we use her as an example of women returning to righteousness? She can no longer confess and repent."

Albert said, "I can tattoo ABORTIONIST on her. We can throw her into the Trevi. A warning."

"Or," Xavier said in a soft tone, "we can bury her out in the vineyard, pray for the mercy of a loving god. Our Lady said many souls go to the fiery furnace because no one prays for them."

The Cardinal looked at Tommaso and said, "Let us depart from the Wild Vines, leave this to the young men, and pray for the Father's guidance on your next steps, Tommaso."

Tommaso nodded. His next steps. The trip down the hillside would be more painful than the one going up. But nothing compared to the agony Trota was facing, burning in hell. And the torment of their failing to save her.

17

FATHER TOMMASO

Tommaso stood at the head of the table. "She died before we could save her from the hellfire her baby-killing cast her into." Tommaso's heart thudded as he visualized the young woman on fire in the vast and red-hot pit, where his own mother still burned to this day.

"The devil had hold of—" A vibration under his feet stopped Tommaso in mid-sentence. He glanced at the wall sconces. The candles flickered wildly.

They were safer down here than above ground. People upstairs in the restaurant would notice it. He glanced over at the tunnel lined with wooden shelving. The olives were packed in dark glass and the Chianti also, but the grappa in clear bottles was shimmering.

An earthquake. He held his breath. Counted to ten. Counted to ten again. The grappa had settled to perfectly still.

"Nothing major," Tommaso said, and nodded at

Roger before he carried on with what had happened to Trota. "The devil had hold of the midwife, body and soul. Her sickness didn't allow Vito's method to work."

He gazed at Vito, who sat with his lips clamped shut, shaking his head, his eyebrows pinched into a dark frown.

Tommaso waited.

Vito's voice was the deepest Tommaso had ever heard it. "A young person like Trota. So rare." Vito turned to Frank. "Did you have any sense of her health issues when you dated her?"

Frank heaved a deep sigh. "On our few hours together, she came across strong. And even more when she carted around all those flyers, nearly forcing people to take them. She seemed robusta, energetic, urging abortions for poor women." His shoulders slumped, and he stared at the men, shaking their heads in silence.

The quiet moment was broken as Pietro ran down the fan-shaped stairs, his face screwed into a squint. "All's okay above. Just a small tremor, but expect aftershocks."

He stood at the opposite end of the table from Tommaso and steepled his long fingers together. "My brothers, think of the good women you love. Let's change people's hearts and minds, align with Meloni's Brothers of Italy. Push to reinstate the law banning abortions."

He looked each man in the face, before he pulled out a chair and sat. "On my podcast, I can lead a public relations campaign. Also flood messages over social media and flyers in cafes, bars, bookstores, women's health settings, and on churches." He drew invisible squares in the air, danced his fingers to indicate words as he said: "Centuries of Catholic Faith. A Family Church. Women are Italy's proud mothers. Be a man. Protect women."

Xavier nodded in agreement. "I'm with you Pietro. I can work on the social media part."

"No," cried Frank. "No one pays attention to soft persuasion. Women like Trota pander to the public about free choice, they support corrupt politicians. They are headed for the flames. They need to be turned around."

"But we risk hell ourselves, if we cause them to die! Don't you see that?" cried Pietro, breathing hard and fast.

Tommaso shouted, "We did not cause her to die! She chose to resist the call to confession and redemption. She chose the devil's side, to kill hundreds of babies and drag other women with her on the road to hell."

The Cardinal stood and smoothed the front of his black cassock. He ran the tip of his index fingernail up and down the scarlet piping. "Demons afflicted Trota," he intoned. "Italy is anointed to protect the faith handed from Jesus to St. Peter, the rock. We live on a battleground, between warring angels and demons. Demons torment our people through the agency of witches."

Roger pounded the table. "Ambitious women hide everywhere among us," he cried. "They don't want males to exercise control over them. This spring, the Carmelite nuns in Texas refused to obey their Bishop. They have been excommunicated."

The Cardinal rubbed his chest, his fingertips zig zagging across his scarlet piping, and he said, "Most nuns respect Holy Church teachings." He held up the *Malleus.* "But women are easily provoked to ambition, and more nuns have expressed envy of priests. The line in the sand is ordaining women as priests, and our pope is under great pressure to step over that line. He is softer than the one before, God rest his soul." He took a deep breath and stood a bit taller. "This current pope smiles on Catholics who want us to become a church 'on the move.'" The Cardinal waved his tattered copy of the *Malleus* in the air and clutched it to his bosom. "On the move! Women priests! Heresy!"

Out of breath, the Cardinal reached to take a strawberry from the bowl. He sat and toyed with the little red berry on his plate.

Tommaso checked the faces of the other men. He was prepared for some heated debate and haggling on how to proceed after their cause had been dealt such a horrific blow with Trota's death.

"Nuns," said Carlo. "They envy priests. I saw one at Giulia's, caught a photo of her on the way to the back room, where women were making posters and singing." He waved his phone in the air, showing the photo of a woman in a black and blue headscarf on the screen.

Tommaso reached to hold Carlo's phone steady a moment. "I talked with Mother Catherine on the phone about this troublemaker. She came to see me. She is smart and not too far gone to get back on the right road. Her name is Sister Fredericka."

"Nuns make men feel like little boys," Carlo said. "Impotent."

The Cardinal chimed in, "For the most part, nuns' discipline helps keep tradition alive. But, I've had reports that demons have taken over some."

Vito fanned his cheeks with his napkin, his eyes wide open and eyebrows lifted nearly to his hairline. Pietro sat with a long face, pulling on his earlobe.

Tommaso stood. "With Mother Catherine's approval, I called Sister Fredericka to my office last week after I saw her on TV, marching with Mary, a bold parishioner of mine. I warned Sister Fredericka that activism in favor of 'attempted ordination' of women is a grave crime under church law, in the same category as sex abuse of minors and heresy."

He paced the floor near the shelving, glancing at the bottles of grappa. "I reminded the sister that diabolical, dark influences are fighting for dominion over our nation. She protested and praised the Pope's openness to change in the church, but I reminded her there are portals to darkness we all have to be vigilant against."

The Cardinal nodded. "We must stand firm against changes that could come out of the October synod. The Pope allowed one nun to participate, even though she is heterodox and publicly does not conform to church teachings. Same as a heretic!" He checked the disturbed faces of the men at the table.

"The good news is there won't be any binding decisions on female deacons nor, heaven forbid, on ordination this year, because it is the first of a two-year process. So, we still have time to make a difference."

Tommaso said, "I suspect that Mary and Sister Fredericka meet to plan activities like supporting nuns becoming priests."

Carlo piped up in a squeaky voice and said, "Some nuns are as bad as abortionists in killing the spirit with harsh discipline. They are like bad mothers opposing the Virgin Mary, our perfect but..." He had tears in his eyes. "Unobtainable mother."

Tommaso's heart contracted over the pain he had suffered from his earthly mother. Beads of sweat formed on his forehead as he visualized the blazing furnace she was locked into.

"The women plan to march and honor Marina the Monk," Carlo said. "After that nun left, I entered the back room to carry out their dirty dishes. They didn't cover up their posters soon enough." He showed his phone screen again. "A sneaky woman who was a monk! The march is on June 17th on the street leading to the Vatican."

The Cardinal said, "Good work, Carlo. We can offer this Sister Fredericka the chance to be corrected and to repent publicly as a leader of women, who under it all yearn to turn away from ambition."

Tommaso said, "Yes, we want to help carry them to the gates of Purgatory where they have a chance to redeem their souls."

Vito poured himself a shot of grappa, then said, "Let's give this woman the opportunity to be corrected when we point out it is heresy against holy church for women to be priests. I will use more traditional HypnoConvert materials this time." Vito turned to Albert. "Can you and Xavier go and divert Sister Fredericka away from that march?"

"Absolutely," said Albert.

Vito raised his grappa and toasted Albert and Xavier. "Blessed sons of the Father!"

The air felt lighter in the cellar. Tommaso welcomed Carlo announcing he had a joke for the Cardinal, if he permitted. The Cardinal gave a half smile and nodded.

"Well," said Carlo, "The Pope died, and they needed a successor. The Cardinals all gathered and considered naming Cardinal Sicola as the new pope, but he was not chosen because they didn't want a Pope Sicola." He raised his glass of Chianti in a toast.

The Cardinal laughed. "That's a good one, my friend. The devil does not like jokes. That's why we must keep our sense of humor. God has one, you know."

Carlo said, "I volunteer to help get Sister Fredericka from the march."

Tommaso replied, "All right, but don't be obvious, just be there to see what Albert and Xavier might need." He turned to Albert. "How will you proceed?"

"We are good at this," said Albert. "I have my special inhalant, more potent than chloroform, with an equal margin of safety. It stops communication between the brain and body, causing unconsciousness. She will fall into our arms."

Tommaso said, "Xavier, post progress reports so I will know what is happening."

The two young men smiled, looking the part of angels, thought Tommaso. He stood to indicate the meeting was over. "God bless you, men of Dei Patris. Vito will help Sister Fredericka set an example for women to embrace the blessedness of their place, equal but different from men, their complementary role in God's—"

A loud thud interrupted Tommaso. A bottle of grappa had fallen off the shelf to the packed dirt floor. Tommaso counted to ten, then to ten again. It was a sign. Time to put the plan into action.

18
HILLARY

The Delta 757 hit a rough patch. A moment of weightlessness hit Hillary, followed by a sinking sensation in her stomach. Out the window, she could see control flaps fluttering at the edge of the wing. She bent forward, clasped her hands against her belly and pinched the Mary medal hanging from her bracelet. They must be over Colorado's Rocky Mountains.

Ed elbowed her. "Normal turbulence, Genevieve." She turned to him, close by her side, the arm rest between them raised back. Thank God she'd taken a Xanax.

He let out a soft whistle. "That's normal, but look at this." He shifted his iPad so she could read it.

Woman found Dead in Trevi

By Angela Narratrice. BBC News• *Updated: Thur - 06/015/2023 - 10:08*

Italian police are hunting for the killer of a young woman discovered early Wednesday in the Trevi Fountain. A barista on his way to work described a slim figure dressed in black carrying something over his shoulder. "He dumped a bundle into the Trevi and ran off onto a side street."

Chamber of Deputies leader Elly Schlein expressed outrage and noted that Italy faces a "surge in femicides." Schlein, a leader in the LGBQ rights movement, reported one of her aides missing after an explosion near the Coliseum during Rome's Pride Parade. "We hope these crimes are not connected." Italy's first female prime minister, Giorgia Meloni of Brothers of Italy, the national-conservative, populist party, declined comment.

HILLARY'S SHOULDERS TIGHTENED. SHE GLANCED across the aisle at Claire seated next to her grandmother. "So proud of her LOVE WINS tee shirts," she whispered. "We've got to keep her safe."

He shook his head. "Claire thinks she's invincible. We have time to talk her out of going away for college in Italy."

Hillary shook her head. "It's that gender studies program the college rep got her excited about. After Claire tours the place, she might see it's not the wonder their website makes it out to be."

The plane lifted and dropped, seemed to fall out from under them, delivering its reminders they were thirty-six thousand feet up in thin air. Hillary pictured God's hands under the belly of the plane and rubbed the face of her Mary medal. She smoothed her hair back and rested her cheek on Ed's shoulder, yearning for solid ground.

AFTER THEY GOT SETTLED AT THE HOLIDAY INN Express, they went out into the muggy New York City afternoon. It was a short walk to Madison Square Garden where Ed was meeting with the head of security for a tour of the famous venue. Ed hoped to pick up ideas to strengthen the trainings he managed for Sacramento's arena. Protecting gay athletes had become a big challenge, requiring facial recognition systems and cybersecurity defense training.

As they neared the entrance to Madison Square Garden, Claire said, "This is where Lisa Leslie played, first woman in the WNBA to dunk."

"But the Knicks," said Ed, "are still playing here while the women got kicked over to Brooklyn at the Barclay."

"Well, yes, but the Liberty is a team I could play

for someday. Don't see the Knicks putting females on their team."

"Team sports," Paisley said. "You sure you are my granddaughter?"

Just then, a man in a Knicks jersey walked by. "How about those Knicks?"

"Miami killed them in the playoffs," retorted Claire.

The man's eyes got big. "You know your NBA, young lady! Where you from?"

"California, on our way to Italy."

"Ah. Bet you don't know much about the game over there."

"You talking about Lega Basket Femminile?" With one finger, she lifted the chain around her neck, pulled out her St. Goretti medal and twirled it. "I'm a point guard, going to basketball camp in Rome."

He laughed and high-fived her. "Go with God, young lady. May all the saints protect you."

Hillary welcomed the warmth from the man's blessing. She had her threat feelers out all the time since last year when Claire came out to Ed and Hillary. Since then, Hillary had expanded her ethnic studies curriculum to embrace the LGBTQ community.

It was going to be a challenge to face discrimination in Italy, still so traditional. Hillary's glow of pride was dimmed by her fear for Claire's safety. Especially since Claire wore every type of rainbow-themed outfit she could find, especially if it combined Pride with basketball. She was not one to hide her light under any sort of basket.

But this was going to be a safe afternoon. Hillary had registered herself and Claire for a Columbia workshop on Gender Issues. Paisley was going on her own to see the new exhibition of forty works by van Gogh at the Metropolitan.

THAT EVENING, THEY GATHERED AT PAULUCCI'S Osteria where Hillary wanted to eat, to compare Italian food and wine at home with what they would find in Italy.

Claire pulled out her phone to take a selfie for Instagram. "Don't say we are on the way to Rome," cautioned Hillary.

"Why not?" Claire got up from her chair to stand between her parents and stretched out her arm to get the shot.

"It's better if people don't know where you are, some people I mean."

"Don't be silly," said Claire. "No one is after me."

"Your mother has a point," said Ed.

"I'm not a baby anymore. Not her little princess. I know how to take care of myself."

"We want you to be safe, want us all to be safe." Hillary's heart was racing, but she raised her eyebrows and smiled.

"You just want to be the perfect mother. Let's get Paisley in the picture. Look like one big happy family." Claire backed up to fit all four of them into the frame.

"Group selfies," Paisley said and turned her head away. "Count me out. At the Met, I saw Caravaggio's painting of Narcissus, where he encircles his reflection with his arms. It symbolizes falling in love with what you can't have."

Hillary felt riveted to her chair. Narcissus. Hillary forced herself to ask, "What do you want that you can't have?"

Paisley glared at Hillary. "The forgiveness of my daughter."

"Don't be ridiculous," replied Hillary. "Look at all I've done for you." Her mouth was so dry, she couldn't swallow.

Paisley stood and leaned forward. "You called me a narcissist. I painted myself standing at the edge of the sea. Alone. I cannot have what I most want, so I prefer being alone."

Paisley had painted herself at the edge of the sea? So many times, Hillary had gone to Ocean Beach alone. Maybe they were more alike than she realized. No. She would never abandon her child. Paisley was a horrible mother. Selfish. The star of her own show, alone on the stage.

Just like now, scooting her chair back, Paisley walked away, in the direction of the women's bathroom.

"Look what you've done," said Claire. She got up and followed her grandmother.

Hillary's vision blurred. Ed pulled out his white handkerchief and handed it to her.

She blinked back her tears, held the handkerchief against her lips, and studied her menu, wordless. All her choices were blurry.

19
XAVIER

It was barely daylight when Xavier knocked on the door of Eleanora's office. Getting no answer, he tried the knob and found it unlocked. He stepped in and saw the landlady busy sliding beads onto a wire.

"Letting you know, we'll be gone until afternoon, but we're expecting company, two extra cars in the courtyard parking," he said.

She didn't look up. "Grazia," she said.

Outside, Xavier glanced at the Lancia's trunk, relieved there were no explosives to carry today. He slipped into the passenger seat of the sedan. He nodded at Albert, behind the wheel dressed in the garb they'd agreed would get Fredericka's sympathy. Albert backed out of the courtyard. They had the three-hour drive to Rome ahead of them. Wouldn't be any police checkpoints today, unless maybe near the Vatican.

Xavier fastened his seatbelt nice and snug, his stomach empty, his brain alert. Taking Trota had gone perfectly, but Fredericka was taller and stronger, going by Carlo's description and photo. There also would not be the huge crowd like at the Pride parade to mask their actions.

He cracked open his window to let out the smoke from Albert's cigarette. At least Albert was considerate enough not to smoke underground when they were working at the monastery. "Let's go over the plan," Xavier said. "West to Florence then the A1 into Rome and onto the Traspontina. Find a side street to park, pointed back in the opposite direction."

"Won't be much tourist traffic. Nobody ever heard of Marina the Monk. Who knew there were trans men back then." Albert gave a falsetto laugh. "Except for Pope Joan," he added.

"We keep pace with the women and sidle up to Fredericka once they've stopped at the end of the march. Draw her aside, then I clap on the cloth, and we whisk her off to the car."

"Sounds tricky, so different from that Trota bitch," Albert said. He tuned to Radio 24 for Intesa Sanpaolo On Air.

Xavier focused on the booming voice from the radio, discussing trends in wealth management. Since he'd moved in with Albert, Xavier was becoming interested in the global business scene. He'd caught a vision, a glimpse of himself becoming successful. He felt a shred of hope to find a woman attracted to him, now that he was a grown man. He closed his eyes, recalling the days when he was a boy outside in the vineyard. He would hold the trailing grape vines against wires along the trellis. Father Joseph would tie the vines on with brown twine or nail some for extra security. It was hot and sweaty labor, so Father Joseph would take him down to the village after the week's work was complete.

He could almost see them again, the young women running their fingertips over vegetables in the market bins, calling out how overpriced was the eggplant or the persimmons. Especially the cuts of beef—they would ask the butcher to slice it thinner, for Bistecca.

"Just for me," a woman would say, batting her long black eyelashes.

Another would shake her shoulders so her white cotton blouse shimmied back and forth over her flesh while she haggled for a better price.

Xavier breathed faster recalling those days. If only one of those darlings would have looked his way.

Albert found a parking spot next to a row of Sycamore trees. Puzzle-shaped pieces of bark on the ground along with the last of the big brown leaves crunched under Xavier's feet as he stepped out onto the sidewalk, into the noontime air, hot and dry as an oven. "It reminds me of the year I spent in California," Albert said. "The classic Mediterranean climate."

Xavier took in the sight of Albert, standing in one of the black tunics they'd bought online. Albert fastened on a white cap and gathered the attached veil near his cheeks, smooth and silky under his plucked eyebrows. Xavier had to bite his lips to keep from laughing.

"Crazy how much we look like women in these outfits." Albert shook his head as Xavier put on his own cap and veil. "Father Joseph told me that nuns have prayers they say as they put on each piece," Xavier said. "Bless these garments, Father, for the greater good of our spiritual warfare."

They walked toward the Conciliazione, the street lined with four-story buildings, a narrow road broadened in the 1930s by Mussolini when he cleared out workers' homes in the neighborhood to build an impressive boulevard for the capital of his Fascist Italy.

Albert looked to the right, along the route to St. Peter's square. "Did you know this Borgo neighborhood is called Vatican City's front yard?"

"Of course I do! You think I never got away from the Abbey?" Xavier bobbed his head in several directions. "Have you noticed among these dozens of flag-waving tour guides there are several priests? We have to hope none of them will come to Fredericka's aid."

Albert nodded toward a short, bald man taking

photos of the street and the souvenir vendors. "Is that Carlo?"

"Yeah." Xavier rolled his eyes. "Kind of goofy how he spied on the women planning the march, but he's the reason we know what Sister Fredericka looks like. Carlo said he'd come help us today but didn't get the nod from anyone at the meeting. Maybe just ignore him."

Xavier was mentally rehearsing his moves. First, they had to spot her from the photo Carlo had taken. Hope she was not right in front, too obvious to any press coverage that way. He would have to move smoothly along next to Albert as Albert went to her side. They would have to wait until the end of the march and hope her friends didn't notice she was missing right away. He would approach her from behind, so she didn't see the cloth coming.

He slid his hand into his tunic side pocket, feeling for the plastic baggie. Albert had prepared a dose that would keep her knocked out for the three-hour drive back. His other side pocket held the balled-up sock he could shove into her mouth if needed. They would carry her off upright between them, bending to her face as if soothing her, in case anyone on the street gave them a second glance on the way back to the Lancia.

Far down the boulevard, Xavier spotted a couple Swiss Guards standing at attention at the entrance to St. Peter's Square. Their black berets and steel-blue uniforms signified the ordinariness of the day.

He turned left and led the way to the massive front doors of Castel Angelo facing the bridge. Straight beyond that stood rows of bookstands and souvenir sellers backed up to the Tiber.

It was 10 o'clock, and Carlo said that the march was to start at 11:00. "We're too early. We can't just stand here. Nuns have to look like they are on their way somewhere."

"Let's walk across the bridge and see if they are gathering." Albert's whispered falsetto made Xavier smother a laugh. He started down the middle of the bridge's wide span, flanked by solid railings preventing anyone from falling into the fast-flowing Tiber.

On a sidewalk at the foot of the railings, vendors had placed things for sale. One man crouched over his setup, displaying tiny trains, each train car showing a letter of the alphabet. He was enticing tourists to buy trains that spelled out the names of children they might take souvenirs home to. Xavier wondered if he might ever have any children.

At the end of the bridge, Xavier pointed down the street. "There they are." A van was parked with its back doors open. A half dozen women were hauling out signs and banners.

A woman with long black hair was yelling to a nun, "Sister Fredericka! Carry this. The one you left with us." A woman in a blue nun's habit took the sign showing an image.

"Okay, that's Fredericka," Albert muttered. "Let's

get back across the river before anyone calls attention to us."

As the marchers crossed the Tiber, Xavier could hear them singing above the metallic jingling of tambourines. Three rows of them came into view—five, then six, then five. Those in front clutched a wide turquoise banner proclaiming: **The Feast of St. Marina the Monk**.

In the second row, each woman carried her own sign.

Ordain Women
Queer Saints: Marina the Monk
Marina, A Transgender Saint
Ordain Women
Phoebe, a "deacon of the church"
-St. Paul
Male and Female, you are all one in Christ.
-St. Paul

In the last row, the middle three carried a banner proclaiming, **"Rome, the women are ready."**

The demonstrators reached the end of the bridge and began singing "One Bread, One Body" as they turned the corner to march along the Conciliazione.

A few reporters and videographers ran in front of the marchers. Xavier noticed Carlo among those taking photos.

Xavier saw Albert nod toward Fredericka in the last row, nearest to them. She carried a small sign with an image labelled Marina the Monk.

Xavier and Albert followed off to the side of the parade until the marchers reached the entrance to St. Peter's Square and stopped.

Albert walked up alongside Fredericka and tugged at her sign. "I like your sign," he said in a falsetto. "We need help in planning our own march."

Fredericka turned to look at him, then back in the direction of her friends. "I can meet you next week," she said, stepping over near the sidewalk. "How do I reach you?" Xavier whirled and clamped the cloth on her face. As her body sagged, she dropped her sign.

Xavier narrowed his eyes at the marchers, but no one turned to see what was happening. Xavier and Albert hustled Fredericka off, silent and limp. No police were in their vicinity, and it was easy to march her along between them, bent toward her as if to be caring for her as they walked the few blocks. No one was near the Lancia, so they laid her unresisting body in the trunk.

As they drove away, Albert said, "No fight in that one. No fun when they don't resist."

Xavier was shocked at the idea of it being fun to carry off a nun, but he kept quiet. He worried she might regain consciousness, maybe start kicking out the brake lights from inside the dark space of the trunk. He watched for police on the way back. But not a checkpoint in sight.

Albert kept Radio 24 tuned in and it was more than an hour before news came on of the disappearance of one of the women marching near the Vatican this afternoon. When protestors discovered one of their group had gone missing, they started shouting for help. A melee ensued and a bystander taking photos was shot and killed. Xavier wondered if that dead man could have been Carlo trying to get photos for Tommaso.

What ever happened next, Xavier knew they had to keep this woman alive. No more bodies to have to throw into the Trevi. They would use the two-man carry to get the nun up the hillside and down into the open lighted space. Much less stressful for her that way.

20
HILLARY

Hillary was relieved to land safely at Leonardo da Vinci Airport and get off the Virgin Atlantic wide body. Out past the gate, they walked by people facing them, in line to catch the morning flight out of Rome. Claire stretched and adjusted her backpack. A tall, mustachioed man leaned to knock against her as he passed by to board. In a loud tone, he said, "No Pride shirts needed in Rome."

Hillary was proud to see Claire ignore him. As they waited to claim their baggage, all eyes were fastened on a TV monitor on the wall. It showed an image of a nun next to a headshot of a bald man, followed by footage of protestors holding signs and a banner near the Vatican.

Hillary read the crawl in English at the bottom of the screen.

Vatican demonstration. Man shot. Casa di San Carlotta nun missing.

"That's where we're staying," she mouthed to Ed. "One of their nuns has been kidnapped!"

IT TOOK AN HOUR FOR THE BUS TO TRAVEL FROM THE airport to the Termini station. Then another hour to figure out which gate Paisley's train to Venice departed from. Hillary asked Paisley, "Why don't you stay with us in the convent a few days? I reserved a suite that sleeps four."

"I've had enough family togetherness," Paisley said. "I've been invited to stay in Venice at the retreat lodgings."

Hillary harbored mixed feelings as she saw her prickly mother haul her two carry-on suitcases onto the train, relief and yet that raw, skinned feeling of being abandoned again.

Claire blew kisses as Paisley waved goodbye and then turned to point at the glass walls of Borri books, a huge store in the middle of the train station. "YouTube showed they have a good English section," she said, tugging on Hillary's shoulder.

"How about we find some shops in Rome instead?" Hillary said. "We've got to find a cab now." After lugging their suitcases and searching, they finally found the taxi stand. A yellow cab with an Italian driver packed them into his taxi and careened over narrow streets, coming within inches of pedestrians.

Hurtling alongside a four-story wall, nearly scraping the leather off the handlebars of a motorcycle it passed, the taxi screeched to a stop just past a set of wooden doors, next to which was fastened a small plaque. It read Casa di San Carlotta, House of Welcome for Pilgrims and Tourists.

Ed paid the driver and helped pull the suitcases from the rear of the taxi and set them near Hillary, who was figuring out how to unlock San Carlotta's doors. It took a combination of pressing keys to talk to someone inside, along with pushing up and down the handle of the door. "Good security," Ed said.

Once inside, they set their luggage on the tiled floor of what seemed a space too small to call a lobby. There was a counter with a veiled nun sitting behind it. Off to her left were dark wooden doors with CHAPEL painted in gold across the top beam. A sign on the front desk gave times for prayer in the chapel and times when the dining room was open for breakfast, plus WiFi information. A hand drawn map of the four-story convent with rooftop garden was on the wall. All the rooms had fans and windows opening to the courtyard, but no air conditioning.

The place was larger than it had seemed from the outside looking at the yellow stuccoed wall, weathered over the years, its face a bland mask over its colorful interior.

"Welcome," the nun said without a smile on her face. "Please sign in."

"We heard about the nun that's gone missing," Hillary said. "How awful."

"Do you have any leads?" Ed asked.

"We are asking for prayers and holding out hope Sister Fredericka will be found soon," said the nun.

The setting seemed serene considering the circumstances, and Hillary was tired. This was Father's Day for them, after all, even though Italy had celebrated St. Joseph and all fathers back in March.

While Ed and Claire bussed the luggage up to their suite on the 3rd floor, Hillary talked to the nun, a petite woman who called herself Sister Pauline. Hillary got directions to the closest cafe, in a nearby neighborhood square. They could walk there, take Ed for a Father's Day meal.

THEIR WALK TO THE SQUARE ALONG THE COBBLED street revealed a shop with casual clothing, shoes and jewelry, custom made on the premises. Mannequins beckoned from the show windows. "Cute heteronorm stuff for you, Mom," said Claire. "Looks like your style of walking shoes and culottes."

"You could check out something yourself, for a change," said Hillary.

Claire gave a quick shake of her head and ruffled her short blond curls. "Cheugy." Then she noticed the sign advertising a "Make Your Own Italian Sandals" workshop. She and Hillary signed up for the two-hour event. Ed would be away at his conference opening night dinner.

At the cafe, Hillary ordered an Aperol Spritzer and a ham and cheese cornetto.

"Cornbread?" asked Claire.

"It's like a croissant."

"I'm having the classic Margherita pizza," Claire said. "What about you, Dad? What do you want for your late Happy Father's Day?"

"I want to relax and not worry about my girl," he said, leaning to kiss Claire on the cheek. "I'll have the Margherita, too. You know," he said, "We aren't that far from the Coliseum near where that woman was pulled out of the Trevi fountain. I've heard extra measures are now in place. Tomorrow at my conference, they'll show us how the Carabinieri and Polizia work the tourist areas." He winked at her. "I'll get a handle on how to keep you safe."

"Oh, Dad! You're as bad as Mom."

"Hey, you two!" said Hillary. "Could we talk about something else for a change? What about going to see the catacombs? That's got to be pretty safe, yes? "

Claire laughed and said, "I'm going to wear my rainbow skull face tee shirt. Some people think it's weird to go see the catacombs, but I want to. I still dream about Sarah, and how she loved Day of the Dead."

Hillary smiled. "I loved celebrating Dia de los Muertos with her." Eight years ago, Claire had lost the loving attention from Sarah, her stand-in grandmother, when Sarah died on a trip to Ireland. "We're going to be just fine, down there tomorrow, staying alive."

21
HILLARY

The next morning, Hillary and Claire slept in. Their tour of the catacombs didn't start until noon. Ed had left early for opening day of the digital forensics conference.

Hillary was happy with their family suite and its large sitting room with three alcoves for beds and closets. She and Claire took their time sorting out things, neither of them mentioning the alcove for Paisley that stood empty.

Hillary looked forward to today's adventure with Claire, just the two of them. Imagining the confines of the catacombs' underground spaces, though, seemed worse than being cooped up in an airplane. She hoped it wouldn't remind her of being buried in that pit last year, trying to rescue her fellow teacher.

Around 11:00, Hillary asked Sister Pauline, on duty again at the front desk, to call them a taxi. As they waited, a pair of uniformed police officers walked through the lobby on their way out.

"Is there a problem?" Hillary asked Sister Pauline.

"Not at all. The police have been working with Mother Catherine, on the investigation."

"Awful. Are there any leads?"

"I can't discuss Mother Catherine's activities, sorry," Pauline said. "But you're welcome to make an appointment to talk with her yourself."

"I understand," Hillary said. She was pretty sure Mother Catherine wouldn't share what she knew with a stranger.

Hillary led the way out to the narrow street to catch their cab, which sped them to the catacomb tour bus meeting place. Within minutes, they were all loaded in, and the bus lumbered along the bumpy Via Appia Antica for a half hour before it reached the church of St. Sebastian.

Inside the church, a short, muscular guide named Niccolo introduced the group of twenty people to what they could expect. In ancient times, he told them, no burials had been allowed in Rome which was why all the catacombs were outside the city limits. After they went down, they had to stay together and not stray. One could easily get lost in the vast network of tunnels, he warned.

Niccolo opened a door leading to a landing above a staircase. He explained they would be walking down four levels before they would go into a tunnel. Still a bit woozy from jet lag, Hillary clutched the cold metal strap of the staircase railing. She lost track of the number of steps as she followed Claire down into a cold open space with a high ceiling. Soon their group moved into a tunnel and Niccolo warned the tall men in the group to bend down so as to not hit the earthen ceiling.

Light bulbs in metal cages had been installed every ten feet, so people could see to make their way along rows of burial niches, gaping open and empty as if still waiting to be filled with a dead body and sealed. "These shelf-like spaces cut into the walls are 'loculi'," Niccolo said. "This catacomb was an ancient burial site, the first to honor St. Peter and St. Paul. Back then it was well known as a site where human and other artifacts could be stolen and sold, and most of the niches have been emptied by looters over the centuries."

"Were people ever walled up in here, like in Poe's story?" a plump man asked.

"Although 'Cask of Amontillado' was based on a true story, no, that was not commonly done," said Niccolo.

"Creepy to be stuck here forever," said Claire. "Almost better to have been carried off somewhere."

Some of the gaping wounds in the side of the earth had name plates beside them. Reading names and dates brought tears to Hillary's eyes. These were real people, their bones now scattered who knew where, over space and time.

Niccolo led them into a large, well-lit space that

struck Hillary as somehow similar to the inside of a spaceship in the movies. He motioned for them to gather around, as he stepped behind a white marble altar. "This place is a 'cubicula,' where memorial services were held for martyrs like St. Sebastian and others."

Hillary was surprised to see such a cavernous space so deep underground and amazed it hadn't caved in after all these centuries. She looked up to study the earthen ceiling, thinly plastered over, and asked Niccolo, "How is it possible that these caverns never cav—"

She crumpled to the ground and everything went black.

22
FATHER TOMMASO

Aching and weary, Tommaso pulled into the courtyard and parked next to Vito's Audi. The man himself was nowhere to be seen. He must have already hiked up the hillside to the abbey. Tommaso felt bound to oversee Vito's process, considering the mess he'd made of Trota's opportunity to repent. They had failed to take into consideration Trota's health, that the rigors of saving her soul might push her over the edge. Of course, he should have realized that, considering how dangerous doing exorcisms was, for all parties concerned. Vito's method was much safer. Or should be for most people. Tommaso felt sure that Fredericka was healthy, but a mix of the two methods could be needed.

The Cardinal was not coming today. He had confessed he feared his leading the project to restore women to what God wanted them to be could become public knowledge after the first attempt went so wrong. The Cardinal kept many of his activities under wraps. And rightly so, thought Tommaso.

The two young men should arrive here soon, bringing Sister Fredericka for her opportunity to return to the true faith. Tommaso would hurry up to the abbey as quickly as his pain allowed. Saving this one soul would make him feel better. Looking for that one lost sheep mattered. Returning her to the fold. Tommaso sat for a few minutes, willing energy for the glory of God the Father to send strength to his legs.

Step by step, Tommaso made his way up the hillside. He rested at each old bench, taking care not to sit where the pine slab had rotted away. When he got up near the church, he stopped and planted his feet wide, to catch his breath and gaze over the shriveled vineyard.

The midday sun soothed his aching muscles. He closed his eyes and drifted back in memory to when he was a teen, one of Father Joseph's orphans tending the grapes. Later, in his twenties, he had moved down to Voce Sotto but came back once in a while. Couldn't recall why. Certainly hadn't helped maintain the pine benches. Waves of heat rose from the rusty grape trellis wires. Tommaso stared at them and shuddered at the faint images of ghosts dancing among the wild vines.

Once inside the church, he paused to rest near the altar, running his fingers through the fringe of his thinning hair. At last, he gritted his teeth, and having no one to light an oil lamp for him, made his way down in the dark, each stair step demanding his concentrated attention. His legs felt stronger once he was on flat ground again.

Tommaso walked through the tunnel. At Father Joseph's tomb, he stopped to press his palm against the clay nameplate. He prayed for the repose of his foster father's soul. The priest had been kind to him. Tommaso groaned, recalling the night he'd discovered his mother dead in an alley. She had started working in an illegal brothel for safety, but it didn't save her.

He focused on the bright open space far off at the end of the tunnel and called out, "Vito! I'm here."

No response. But Vito must be here. "Vito! Can you hear me?" Nothing. He called again and heard a slight echo. Maybe there were more rooms than he'd noticed that time before with Trota.

He stood in silence. Today would be a shock for Sister Fredericka, but a blessing, too. A-chance to turn her life around. He'd learned from his phone calls with Mother Catherine that Fredericka was probably not possessed, but those words coming out of Fredericka's mouth about women sounded diabolical. She was clearly heretical. Mother Catherine never accused Fredericka of heresy, but there was a special quality in Catherine's tone of voice over the phone that Tommaso recognized as a pure-in-heart concern, a worry. Or was it fear?

Tommaso walked with a limp to the edge of the open lighted place, thinking he needed to buy himself a cane. The big worktable was over to the side, and two pieces of furniture he'd never seen before stood next to it, facing each other.

With no warning, Vito appeared. "Hello!"

Tommaso waved his arm toward where Vito had come from. "Where were you?"

Vito slapped one of his big hands against the other. "I must have stirred up some dust!" He sneezed. "This place goes on a couple more rooms, the last one has niches sealed up long ago." He jerked his head towards where he'd come from. "The room next to us has an altar."

"I'm not surprised," Tommaso said. "Many catacombs have spaces for services honoring the departed." He turned in the direction of the long table. "Tell me about this new set up."

"I moved the table over to make more space. Then I hauled some things up from my car. A nice rug. A zero-gravity lounge chair for Fredericka's comfort. A folding camp chair will work for me or when you need to sit, the times you're here with us."

Afternoon sunlight from an air shaft streamed over the three-piece grouping of furniture. Tommaso eyed Vito as the psychologist went on describing his plan. "We'll talk face to face, a normal therapeutic setting. I've got a chamomile incense stick going, help her relax. Not to mention passionflower tea."

Vito stood tall and confident. His deep voice, dark brown hair and brown eyes reminded Tommaso of a substantially built opera singer, maybe a Pavarotti in his ordinary off-stage life.

Despite the tragedy with the abortionist, and Tommaso prayed that her soul had, against all odds, made it to Purgatory, Tommaso still trusted Vito. The man had won prizes for best practices teaching therapeutic hypnosis, his voice was soothing, his gestures, fluid. He came across as a man you could count on, confident without being abrasive.

"You could have been good at giving homilies, had you been called into the priesthood," Tommaso told Vito.

Vito nodded. "We are a team. Brothers of the same Father, working to save Fredericka from the demon inside her."

Tommaso walked to the chair for Fredericka and rubbed his palm across the top of its back as if blessing it. "You're putting her in a lounge? What if she wants to sit up?"

"That is one of the positions it can go in, yes."

"What if she runs up the stairs and out into the vineyard?"

"She's a nun. God protects her, a dignified woman even though she's radical. She won't run. We'll test her out at first, of course."

This assessment fit Tommaso's sense of the nun. "Where will the young men be while you and I work with her?"

"We can start out together, but then you can leave her to me. That's what I was getting that other room ready for. You can rest yourself in one of the folding chairs there. I've set out preparations. Albert and Xavier will leave us alone. They said they can settle themselves in the old monastery workroom where Xavier bakes his bread. They'll be nearby if needed."

Tommaso nodded. "Go on."

"You can explain at first how this is for Sister Fredericka's benefit, and she can serve as an example for others. If she agrees to slip into trance, or even if she resists, I'll be focusing suggestions on the desired outcome."

Tommaso nodded. "I learned from Mother Catherine that Fredericka recently returned from caring for her mother in her final days. You can suggest her mother approves of her repenting."

Suddenly, there she was, standing tall in the open lighted space, her red hair flowing and green eyes flashing, unbowed by the black and blue paisley scarf binding her arms together at the wrists. She sang out in a rich contralto that surprised Tommaso. "Which mother do you mean?" It was so different from her ordinary voice.

"Buongiorno!" Tommaso tried to match the energy in her tone. "Your mother. I learned that you were in the US last year, caring for your mother in hospice. God rest her soul." Not a muscle moved on Fredericka's face.

Vito nodded at Xavier and Albert, standing behind her. "Thank you for getting her safely up here.

You can go now, to the Abbey. Make us some of your bruschetta." They took the hint and departed.

"Come have a seat. Relax," Vito said. Fredericka stood, still as a statue.

Tommaso walked closer to the nun. "Mother Catherine said she was concerned about the time you spent in America with an Episcopalian priest, a woman named Meghan. She told me you returned to Rome a bolder woman than when you'd left." Tommaso frowned. "I hope you realize that marching in public at the Vatican for the ordination of women priests is heresy. It was all over the media."

He waited.

The nun made no response. Had she gone mute?

"Remember that special day when you lay prostrate under the black pall of death?" He spread his arms out toward the rug. "Visualize yourself there, dear sister, taking your final vows." He bowed his head and closed his eyes. "You begged the Lord to grant you the grace of never offending Him by even the smallest sin, yet look what you have done."

He raised his head and looked at her. She was staring straight ahead at one of the empty niches. "You were promised that the Lord would enlighten you whenever you strayed even one inch."

Tommaso smiled at her. "We are here in His name, caring for you for your benefit, to save your soul. You can be a light to others. Die to your own ambition. Return to the Father's grace. Do you hear me?"

No reaction from her. “Listen to us,” Tommaso said and nodded at Vito.

Vito cleared his throat and waved her toward the recliner. “I’m Vito Gallo, a spiritual director. Please sit and relax.”

Fredericka moved toward the recliner but veered off to the long table.

Vito said, “Let’s talk this over like sisters and brothers in the Lord. I find it can be beneficial to use trance as a way in to fruitful conversation, if you’ll allow?”

She lifted her arms bound at the wrist and rapped her knuckles on the tabletop. “I’d like you to untie my scarf, please, and certainly not to hypnotize me.”

“Of course!” Vito undid the knot and laid the scarf on the rich wood surface. Fredericka rubbed her wrists and smiled at Tommaso. “Such an unusual place to meet up with you, Father.”

He gulped, his throat dry, wishing he had a cup of water.

She stretched the scarf out on the diagonal and snapped it into a triangle then laid it across her forehead and fastened it at the back of her neck. “No offer of an afternoon coffee, gentlemen? I’m quite thirsty, that long ride, shut up in the trunk.”

“Mi scusi,” said Vito. “I can’t offer expresso but do have herb tea.”

“Yes, please, and water.” She retraced her steps and sat in the camp chair.

Vito carried on smoothly without telling her she was sitting in his chair. "Father," he said to Tommaso, "please confer with our visitor while I prepare refreshment."

Tommaso avoided Fredericka's cool gaze as he grappled with the recliner for a few minutes before he managed to get it into the upright position.

He sat and spoke in an earnest tone. "Now, Sister, do not fear. You are here because we bear the love of God the Father to you. As you know, I am acquainted with all forms of heresy and its consequences." Tommaso found himself short of breath. The incense. It never used to bother him.

He had to close his eyes a few moments and take a deep breath before he continued. "Because of your actions, in disobedience to the Church, it is with deep sorrow…" He frowned, squinted at her, and pressed one hand over his heart. "I may have to inform the faithful that you have incurred upon yourself excommunication."

He stared at her, intent on impressing her with the gravity of her action, and she stared back, not moving a muscle. "Did you hear me? Excommunication." The six syllables came out slowly, and hung in the air.

Her response was an occasional blink of her eyelashes. How could she remain so still? He could hear liquid being pouring in the other room and felt he'd perish of thirst.

"You do understand our Holy Mother Church

teaches it has the power to ordain men to the priesthood because Jesus called men to that service. Women have other ways to serve. Especially as a Catholic nun, your work is to support Christ's great church, the scriptures and traditions. In all obedience."

She sat staring, a slight smile on her face, the perfect oval of its shape emphasized by the contours of the edges of her scarf.

Tommaso found her silence unnerving. "It is important that you say if you understand the church teaching. Do you?"

She rolled her lips in, making them disappear into her mouth, lowered her gaze and closed her eyes, as if possessed with a demon like the mute man Jesus healed. She wasn't speaking.

Drops of sweat ran down Tommaso's back, into the crack of his buttocks. He fingered the silver cross hanging from the black cord around his neck. Maybe he should have brought along some holy water.

Vito reappeared and set an expresso cup on the long table next to Fredericka. "Please. Enjoy the tea."

Tommaso noted Vito had not brought the water she had asked for, along with the tea. He hoped there was water in the other room.

Vito turned to Tommaso. "Let us give Sister Fredericka," Vito spoke in a slow monotone, "the opportunity to be corrected. It is heresy against holy church teaching for women to be priests." He nodded at Tommaso.

That was his cue to remind her again of what

should be second nature to her. Tommaso swallowed and wished for a glass of water but didn't want to veer from the way Vito had started. "Yes. The Church must judge heretics by outward signs like Sister Fredericka marching for women's ordination in public at the Vatican." He shook his head. "But if a heretic returns to the Holy See's traditions, she is to be received as a penitent heretic. Then we can again bless her for embracing the one true church that Jesus founded with the rock, Peter, at the head and men as priests."

Fredericka took the small cup and sipped at the cooled tea over the next few seconds, wordless. Then she said in a low tone, almost a whisper, "I listen and follow God's will. He sent me here to play devil's advocate."

Tommaso gasped. She could talk. It wasn't a demon keeping her silent. She was admitting she was spewing forth the voice of the devil. "This is serious, to save your soul and by example, save other women, as well." Tommaso felt dragged by intense thirst out to the other room. "I'll give you time to think about it, pray about it." He nodded at Vito, standing near her, and he left the open lighted space.

In the other room, a thermos, some paper cups and a gallon jug of water stood on an altar. Under the thermos was a note saying, "For Fredericka only." Tommaso poured himself half a cup of water from the jug and chugged it down.

He returned to the open lighted space and patted

the back of the lounge chair. "Please, Fredericka, move to the comfort of this lounge."

With both hands, she smoothed her scarf down, cupping the fabric and holding it pressed against her ears. She shook her head. Tommaso sighed and gingerly sat on the lounge, casting a doleful look at Vito.

Vito pulled out a folding chair from the long table. He positioned himself with Fredericka at his left and Tommaso at his right. He spoke in slow and soothing tones. "Now relax and listen, Sister. You are safe here. Recall all that you've learned in your journey. The scriptures do not permit women to exercise headship. It is contrary to the character of God's act in creation. Isn't that right, Father Tommaso?"

Tommaso nodded and cleared his still dry throat. "The Church has no authority to ordain women. I know you understand the scriptural basis for this, Fredericka, and yet you have the indwelling spirit of envy." He stopped for a few seconds. "The demon of envy made you march in defiance of holy church, not accidentally or out of ignorance."

She raised her eyebrows and tilted the small cup, draining the last of the tea. "It is true I am informed about the church's choice of what to teach, but my difference of opinion on this point is not heresy."

"Well," said Tommaso, wishing he had water at hand, "it's not that the church chooses not to ordain women, it's that the church is unable to ordain women because Christ did not give his church the authority to do that. The church imitates Christ who chose only men to be apostles."

Vito added, "And Jesus did include women within his circle. Blessed women." His voice was low. "His mother, Mary, the God bearer…" Tommaso noted Vito was speaking slowly, pausing for each word to sink in. "She whom we adore with each breath." He paused and breathed in and out audibly. "She deserves the highest praise. And yet not even Mary the mother of God was chosen to be an apostle."

Fredericka took her small cup in hand. She said, "Apostle simply means messenger." She pounded the empty cup against her palm as if it were a gavel. "The story of leadership in the early church is complicated. St. Paul greeted Phoebe as deacon and Junia as an apostle. Even back in the fourth century, the bishop of Constantinople granted the femininity of Junia."

Vito said, "But listen. Slow down and listen to yourself. You cite Paul and Bishop Chrysostom. They are not Jesus. Visualize our Lord. Two thousand years ago. Breathe it in. Two. Thousand. Years. Men in the priesthood. The Church's teaching and practice is free from error. Opposing it is heretical."

Fredericka's eyelids drooped.

Tommaso stood and took a deep breath. He wondered if the incense and tea were having an effect on her. He plunged in with his key concern. "You are envious of men, Sister. Envy is like the sin of personal ambition. Centuries ago, we were warned that witches were infected with ambition. Today, craving for power rises among women. Envy is a grave sin. A mortal sin."

Tommaso felt woozy, almost sedated by his own slow and soft voice in the smoky atmosphere of the space, now growing dark as evening came on. Hearing no response from Vito or Fredericka, he continued. "A person who dies in mortal sin cannot enter the kingdom of heaven and is doomed to eternal suffering in hell. There is no chance to purify in Purgatory."

Fredericka stared at the earthen wall across from her, with no expression on her oval face. Was a demon shutting her up?

Vito said, "Envy. It's human. Sisters envy brothers. We are all sinners."

Tommaso waited in the silence. It was his duty to remind her what she already knew. "All sins can be forgiven. If you repent and turn away from the heresy of women priests, I am ready to offer the Sacrament of Reconciliation for forgiveness of your sins. Jesus gave the power to forgive sins in his name. I remind you what he told his apostles: 'Receive the Holy Spirit. Whose sins you forgive are forgiven them, and whose sins you retain are retained.' The priests of the Catholic Church forgive sins in Jesus' name."

Fredericka stood and walked to the wall. She turned to face them, her hands extended as if in greeting. "Gentlemen. Something which once seemed of the utmost importance can suddenly seem of no significance, as if it had never been." She ruffled the lose folds of her habit. "Let me point you to a key example: the Christian ban on menstruating women from participation in the sacraments or even from approaching the altar."

---

23
HILLARY

Hillary lay resting in the quiet of the suite. Ed was at his conference keynote dinner. Claire had gone to the nearby make your own sandal workshop and let Hillary take it easy. Hillary was lucky.

Niccolo had been unruffled at her fall. He made the others step back and give her room. She was not the first to faint in the narrow passages. He explained that falling down started its own recovery because being flat let more blood flow to the brain.

It took less than a minute before Hillary was able to stand back up. The tunnels had brought back the time of being thrown into that walnut orchard pit. She'd been working to free her colleague and got trapped herself. Today, she'd been sweaty from the enclosed spaces and from the memory, too. Claire had stayed by her side the rest of the tour.

Hillary realized she could make it to evening

prayer at 6:00 if she hurried. Divine consolation sounded good. She prayed no more catacombs for her.

The chapel was larger than she'd imagined. Four rows of pews faced an altar. Fresh red roses in a clear glass vase stood on a small stand by a lectern. A faint fragrance hung in the air. A single candle stood at the side of the altar.

She took a seat in one of the narrow wooden pews and pulled a book from the little rack in front of her. She thumbed through the book. It was in Italian. How would she be able to follow along? The nun she'd met at the front desk was there, in a pew next to Hillary's. Sister Pauline. Without a word, the young nun gestured toward the book in Hillary's hand. Hillary offered it to her. The nun opened it. She ran her fingertip under a line near the top of a page and looked to see if Hillary understood. That must be where they would start the service. Hillary nodded and Pauline handed the book back to Hillary.

Hillary could translate a few of the words Pauline had pointed to. *Padre Nostro. Padre.* That must mean Our Father. The Lord's Prayer.

Two other nuns entered and seated themselves in front of Hillary and Pauline. Another sister entered from a side door and lit the candle. At the lectern, she opened a book and started reading aloud, "Padre Nostro," while the other nuns voiced along with her.

Hillary followed the prayer in Italian. *E rimetti a noi i nostri debiti.*

Debiti. That must be debts. Debts. Trespasses. Forgive us our trespasses, she thought.

Come noi li rimettiamo ai nostri debitori. As we forgive those who trespass against us. Forgive those. It was her mother who trespassed against her, running out on her. How could she forgive her?

She found it hard to swallow, her throat dry. Here in this hot summer, in a foreign language, the crucible of forgiveness surrounded her.

Her stomach growled. Sister Pauline glanced her way and smiled.

A lump grew in Hillary's throat. She knew she had to get over holding this grudge, but she couldn't forgive Paisley until she heard her say she was sorry.

IN THE LOBBY, HILLARY FOUND SISTER PAULINE NOW sitting at the front desk. There were only the two of them at the moment. Hillary said, "On my BBC app, I read an update about the kidnapping, and I wondered if I might be able to help. I was a reporter, and I've helped investigate missing person cases."

Pauline looked around the small space, closed her eyes for a moment, crossed herself and leaned forward. "I think Fredericka might be being punished for promoting women's ordination in public," she whispered.

Hillary bent closer to catch her words, as the nun continued. "I feel guilty. I encouraged her activism through my work, although my project is private."

"Your project?"

"I'm working on a new edition of the Bible, but nothing to march out in the streets and get punished for."

Hillary said, "Punished?"

Pauline whispered, "Mother Catherine got word that people are trying to get Fredericka to confess and ask for forgiveness."

Hillary's mouth dropped open. "People? Who?"

Pauline shook her head. "I don't know, but that *Daily Bread* podcast is asking Mother Catherine to go public and urge Fredericka to repent and lead a demonstration on traditional family values."

"Unbelievable," said Hillary.

Pauline frowned. "Mother Catherine would do nothing of the kind. It's the traditionalists," she whispered, "combating the progress since Pope Francis was elected. I think they are behind the kidnapping."

"Has Mother Catherine talked to the authorities?"

"Yes, of course."

"I'm praying Fredericka is safe and will be found soon," Hillary said. She liked the new pope and kept her Mary medal attached to her bead bracelet, but a few years ago, she and Ed had left and become Episcopalian. Claire still went occasionally to Catholic Mass where they'd had her confirmed the summer she turned seven. Tomorrow, the three of them were scheduled to tour the university Claire was so eager to attend. It wasn't Catholic, but Hillary wondered if Claire might find it was still too conservative for her.

24
FATHER TOMMASO

Tommaso's heart raced. He had heard of this but thought it was just rumor. Fredericka carried on. "This time of the month prohibition, which seems so bizarre to us now, is first encountered in the bishop of Alexandria's writings, at the beginning of the third century."

Vito stood tall, silent, his eyes open wide as the nun carried on.

"One of few exceptions to this denial of women's equality was granted by Pope Gregory, soon after launching his mission to England under the monk Augustine. The pope's open-mindedness was probably caused by his irritation with the Christians already in Britain who resisted his papal authority. These native Christians were rigorous against menstruating women, and it was their independent mindedness that provoked the pope's ruling against them."

Tommaso was dumbfounded. Fredericka was giving a sermon.

"The consensus against menstruating women began to fade in the Reformation, among Protestants whose worship was less centered on the sacraments, but the prejudice survived in parts of Lutheranism and Anglicanism until the 1950s," she said.

Tommaso was finding her story hard to believe.

Fredericka rubbed the flat of her hands against the cloth of her habit, in long ovals over her thighs, then said, "In fact, in 1970, a regulation of the Catholic church still excluded women lectors from the sanctuary during their periods."

Tommaso crossed his arms over his chest and deepened his frown. Fredericka stepped closer to him. "So, talk to me about two thousand years of male only priests, when after seventeen hundred years, the Church changed her mind about keeping menstruating women out of the sanctuary."

Tommaso couldn't think of anything to say. Vito was silent, his jaw hanging open.

Fredericka nodded with a slight smile on her lips. She stood and stretched, then rubbed her belly. "In fact, I need you to provide me with feminine hygiene products. Soon."

Tommaso couldn't stand the sight of blood. They'd overlooked this issue.

"Yes." She nodded. "We women can feel into the recesses of our 'gut brains'—our womb space—and the intelligent temples of our hearts to access insights, intuitions, and sacred knowing.

"When we are fully present, grounded, aware and heart-centered, we access authentic spiritual, mental, and physical power. Using our voices becomes natural, and swallowing our anger isn't an option. Like we spoke out when we marched in Rome. When we are in our bodies, we are unstoppable."

Tommaso found his voice. "Your body. That is what you are so angry about. You are named after your father Fredrick and jealous of the role God gave men. The tenth commandment tells you not to covet what others have."

"Such as testicles?" she shouted. "A man's penis and balls give him spiritual power? An accident of birth!"

Tommaso was shocked at the nun's frankness. What could he say?

Vito hummed lightly for a few seconds before he rushed to reply. "Consider how God created all things. Humans. Trees. Some trees are evergreen, some lose their leaves in a rhythm, a pattern over time. They never compare themselves to the others. Would they be envious? Each kind is just right. Same with humans."

He stopped for a few seconds of silence and resumed a low, slow pace. "Male. Female. Valued. Loved. Complementary." He hummed a tuneless drone. "Make no mistake, we need women in the

Church—without them, we would see the downfall of Western civilization."

After a long minute he waved her to sit back down. Tommaso was relieved that she followed Vito's suggestion, and she crumpled into the chair.

Vito closed his eyes and nodded before he spoke again. "Young souls like to rebel. You are rebelling, Sister. Acting out to spite the rules. Be with your inner rebel woman. Soak in the bath of envy." She was slumped forward in the camp chair, her eyes closed.

Vito got up and motioned Tommaso into the other room.

Tommaso could barely make it there. The air full of incense, the light gone, his stomach growling. Vito pulled out some cold pizza from his supply chest. "Eat." He poured water from the jug. "Drink. Let her sit with her thoughts."

Although hungry, Tommaso couldn't take a bite, but he drank down a cup of water.

When Tommaso and Vito reentered the open lighted space, Fredericka called out in a clear tone, "Kidnapping is a mortal sin. It's a crime, too. What you have done to me is but a speck in the system of keeping women down. The patriarchy needs to be destroyed."

Tommaso said, "I offer you the chance to be corrected and to repent publicly as a leader of women, who under it all, yearn to turn away from the heresy of ambition and envy. I suggest as a penance you organize a counter demonstration, promoting the complementary roles of women in the church."

She chuckled and held out her cup. "I'll have more of that tea, please, Mr. Vito."

Vito took her cup and beckoned Tommaso back into the other room.

"I don't like the way this is going," Tommaso said.

Vito nodded. "Yes, it will take more with this woman. Tomorrow, I'll bring a blend of passionflower and valerian tea. Get her to visualize herself as radiant in serving the body of Christ in her role as a blessed bride of Christ."

He nodded toward the earthen side wall in the other room. "I've got the niche prepared for her comfort overnight. I can take in extra linen strips in case she really is about to start her period. That may have just been part of her drama. We better ask Albert to administer his aerosol now. Let her rest overnight and resume our process tomorrow."

Tommaso was sweating. Maybe they wouldn't be able to turn Fredericka around. How much time did he have left?

He would leave Vito here to work with the nun. He would call another meeting. Dei Patris needed a younger, more malleable woman. Build up the body of Christ.

They had to be careful. His headache was killing him. "I'll go now. On my way out, I'll call the young men in to help you," he said.

Vito nodded, bent over a supply chest, gathering fresh linen for the niche.

On the church steps outside, Tommaso took shallow breaths of the warm night air. Dead tired, he stared at the dry vines clinging to the wooden scaffolding, his eyes crossing, a vision forming. Someone was lying there under the vines. It couldn't be. He blinked and rubbed his eyes. Nonsense. Nothing but shriveled leaves. He reached to touch a raisin, a leftover forgotten fruit. They used to get Chianti from these grapes. Now there was nothing but dry sticks. And secrets faded to dust.

25
HILLARY

The three of them taxied from Casa di San Carlotta across the bridge over the Tiber. Hillary had already seen the American University campus, courtesy of YouTube, and knew there wasn't one main campus. Instead, the private school had what the video called a network of learning centers scattered around the Transvere district. The tour would include hiking to the various locations, so Hillary had worn her Adonis sneakers, comfy for all day on her feet.

On this warm morning in June, she felt herself in sync with the past as she got out of the taxi and followed the low stucco fence along the curve of the Tiber, energized by its riffles on the surface

Ancient buildings stuccoed in oranges and creamy pinks faced the river. Despite their coats of many-colored graffiti, the buildings struck Hillary as satisfied with their place in history alongside bookstands, coffee shops, and gelato parlors crowded with tourists. She stopped at a street cart and bought a slice of *pizza al taglio*, the bubbly crust luring her to an after-breakfast snack, although Ed and Claire resisted.

A vendor waved a black silk fan in Hillary's direction. She looked at her daughter. "Want one for a souvenir?"

"No, Mom!" Claire said. "We're here to meet Violet, see the school, not get souvenirs." She kept walking.

Hillary stopped for a second to look at one for herself, a dark blue with a scattering of white flowers, but she hurried away to catch up with the others. They followed the Tiber another block until they found the university buildings facing the river. They were to meet up with Violet Bianchi in the newer of the two buildings. Claire had connected with the woman last year in San Francisco at a fair for study abroad programs and degree seeking students.

The foyer had been redone with a lot of marble. Near the front doors stood a wiry and athletic looking woman, black hair tied low at the back of her neck, who could have been anywhere between 50 and 70. She called out "Hello, I'm Violet, and you must be Claire's family." She greeted Hillary and Ed with kisses on each cheek and put an arm around Claire's shoulder. "Welcome, my young chick, let me take you under my wing!" She winked at Hillary.

Hillary was glad Violet knew Claire had been in an accelerated high school program. She wouldn't be

16 until August and 17 when she started college. She needed to be accompanied by a rep or at least in the company of older students.

Violet carried on in a loud voice, "This area we're in, called the Transvere, is so special. All of Rome is our classroom, but this building..." She waved her arm, inviting them to look up. The open stairwell was bounded by square steel railings rising in a tower to a pyramid skylight at the top. "This building forms a beehive of classrooms alongside the building next door, with courtyards holding umbrella tables and rhododendron climbing the walls."

"I know you are interested in our Gender Studies program, Claire." Violet motioned them to an elevator and once they were all inside, she hit the button for floor 3.

Violet led them down the hall. "Dr. Sterling's office is here. She's in on Tuesdays and Thursdays in the regular semesters. It's becoming a challenge to get into her classes due to growing interest in the field." Violet led them to a bulletin board, plastered with information about events planned for the late summer and into the fall.

"What about the surge of opposition to Gender Studies?" Ed asked. "I know Italy's last election boosted the right wing's success," said Ed.

Violet smiled. "We are not experiencing any push back here on campus," she said. "Let's go next door, have a bite in the new cafeteria."

After they had a snack in the modern building,

Violet led them outside. “Ten minutes behind these buildings is our headquarters, the oldest building of those that make up the campus. It’s near the famous Gate in the old *Aurelian* Walls. They surround the historic center of Rome and are the longest and best-preserved ancient walls in the world. There is even a small pyramid as part of the wall, built two thousand years ago to protect Rome from warring tribes. There’s a Protestant cemetery there now, too.”

Violet pointed out the way to an ancient foot bridge over the river leading to Tiber Island in the middle of the river. “Getting lost can be part of the adventure, but don’t go alone, be with another person at all times,” Violet advised Claire. “Always stay in text contact with your family. The media creates unnecessary worry. It’s very safe here, even though it’s kidnappers on every corner, if you believe some of the news.”

“How close are you to where that nun was taken?” asked Hillary.

“That happened across the river, down by the Vatican, not here in Transvere,” said Violet. “It’s true there are places where being out and proud is safer than others, but you can easily recognize gay-friendly places by rainbows on shops and cafes.”

She led them down sidewalks alongside graffiti-sprayed buildings and pointed out ancient fountains around several corners, some still pouring out water from the working aqueducts. They were nearly side-swiped by cars and taxis whizzing by in the crowded tourist district.

Violet waved to a pair of two-story buildings. "Our residence living is in these apartments. Our students have to be 18 to live here, or otherwise you could start this fall, Claire, dear heart!"

Violet circled back and passed a bookstore set under an archway, a sign boasting of their on-site printing press. Books were stacked on boxes out on the sidewalk. Amid the friendly clutter, the aroma of paper and ink had made it out the double doors all the way to the cobblestone street. Hillary and Claire stopped to inhale the smell they loved.

Once they were back inside the foyer of the modern campus building, Violet waved to a slim, bald man walking by, dressed in a tropical-weight Italian blazer. "Meet Professor Frank, a Medieval Studies scholar," she said.

"Delighted to make your acquaintance," Frank said, giving a formal bow. "If I may be so bold, I see you've given St. Goretti a place of honor," he said to Claire.

"She protects young athletes." Clair lifted the medal and kissed it. "I'm here for basketball camp and to look over the campus. Hope to come here for college next year."

"Splendid! Make sure to take my Divine Comedy class if you want to learn how to get to heaven." He chortled and looked at Violet to laugh with him at the joke he was known for at the school.

"We are on our way up to the weekly meeting of the Queer Alliance," Violet said primly. "Introduce Claire to her community."

Professor Frank scowled. "Now that is the way to take Claire down. The inferno direction."

Violet smiled. "Claire has chosen. It's still a free country, Professor."

She led them over to the elevator. "Don't mind him, he's working on becoming a curmudgeon while he's still young."

Up in the student activities office, Violet introduced them to a half dozen students in the small conference room, and to the leader of the group, Jason Daniels, standing a head taller than the others.

Jason said, "You're welcome to join us for pizza on Friday, Claire." He adjusted the green beret he wore tilted at an angle over his long hair colored a bright turquoise. "We'll be celebrating that final exams of the summer session are over. Party time."

Violet nodded. "Jason is a graduate student, about to enter our doctoral program and teach an art history class in the fall. That's his award-winning work." She waved her hand at a pair of paintings on the wall. One showed a Madonna figure holding a full-grown woman across her lap in the style of the Basilica's famous Pieta. Side by side was a Madonna with a dark baby on her lap, both dressed in white eyelet with big pink bows on their heads.

"You painted Jesus as a girl?" blurted Hillary. She clapped her hand over her mouth.

The room expanded into silence.

Ed's eyebrows flew up to nearly meet his hairline.

Her gray eyes wide, Claire stared at Hillary, then said, "Don't mind my mother, please. So heteronorm."

Her own flaming hot face berated Hillary. Where had that remark come from? If she'd only stopped at that vendor's and bought a dark blue silk fan to hide behind now. There was no hiding from the scorn she saw in Claire's eyes.

26
FATHER TOMMASO

Tommaso's head ached. Another hot day. Should have worn his cassock. He was sweating in his black wool suit. His trousers were sagging. He leaned against the stone wall, hitched them up, and tightened his belt a notch. He must have lost weight.

There were his brothers, below, seated at the long table. There was no food or drink on the table today. It was just as well. His stomach was doing its new slow burn.

At the head of the table, Roger was scowling and thumbing through his phone. Pietro glanced up from his laptop, wide-eyed, the face of God's blessed.

Tommaso made his way down the intaglio staircase, grateful no one seemed to notice his jerky process. He sat and caught his breath before he forced himself to stand. After a deep breath, he said, "Look at us. Gathered in His name, struggling to battle the devil and loosen his grip on our people." The others gazed at him solemnly.

"The mission to save Sister Fredericka's soul is going slowly, I am sorry to report. The situation was smooth at first, but Carlo being shot dead in the Marina March has triggered an investigation of him and his sister Giulia's Cafe." Tommaso sighed. "It could cause us a problem."

On his drive home, Tommaso had reflected on the fact that a Detective Rossi and her partner Mario had questioned Giulia yesterday. Rossi had called and expressed sympathy over the death of Carlo and then asked a lot of questions. What might Carlo have told his sister? Surely not about the meetings at Pietro's?

Tommaso searched his memory. What did Carlo know about the Wild Vines? Yes, he was at the meeting when Albert and Xavier came and talked about Wild Vines as a remote getaway for women to reflect and discern. What all had Carlo told Giulia? What had Giulia told the detective?

"His body won't be released for a while. Let us pray for him now." Tommaso bowed his head. "Eternal rest grant unto your servant Carlo, O Lord, and let perpetual light shine upon him. May his soul and the souls of all the faithful departed rest in peace, through the mercy of God the Father. Amen."

Tommaso crossed himself and said, "Fredericka is proving a stubborn case. She's got a mind, could have taught theology at a university. We've made no progress. Vito is continuing to work with her. That was more important than his coming with me today. But we agreed that a younger, more pliable woman might be more willing to accept our guidance. The Cardinal has chosen to stay in the shadows, aligned with tradition."

Frank took the *Malleus* from his backpack and slammed it on the table. "Tradition?" He pounded his fist on the closed book. "Do you know what departure from tradition the Pope will announce soon? He will announce the church is having priests bless same-sex couples. What do you say to that, Father? How is blessing homosexuality keeping to tradition?"

Tommaso shook his head. Even laymen like Frank had heard the rumors. Tommaso's gut burned. He needed to buy some of those Galeffi effervescent lemon-flavored sticks. Easy to add to water.

Frank opened the book and tapped on a page. "Here we read that witches turn people gay: they stir up hatred between married couples so they cannot perform the reproductive function, and in the night, men and women search for irregular lovers."

Tommaso nodded. "St. Paul wrote a letter to our Roman ancestors. He said God gave sinners over to 'shameful lusts… women traded natural sexual relations for unnatural ones… men abandoned relations with women and were inflamed with lust for each other'."

Frank's eyes bulged. He forked his fingers through his hair and made it stand on end.

Tommaso had no answer. What was the pope thinking?

"And in that vein," continued Frank, "a new class is being offered where I teach." He pulled his phone out from the breast pocket of his white summer suit. "Topics include gender identity, gender role socialization, sexual orientation development, and…" he paused before shouting, "parenting!"

He waved his phone in the air. "Parenting! What kind of children can queer parents raise?"

Tommaso fanned himself with the sides of his black suit jacket. How did Frank stay looking so young and fresh when he was fired up with such Godly passion?

Pietro smiled and leaned forward. He positioned his laptop to face the others. "I've got some good news. The podcast I launched last month, "*Daily Bread —Give us this Day*," is adding hundreds of subscribers each day." He pointed to the computer screen showing the title of the podcast spread across an image of people at a banquet table loaded with bread and wine.

Tommaso placed his hands on his belly and pressed lightly to settle the pain, as Pietro continued. "Media experts tell me it's growing at the rate Rush Limbaugh's show grew, back in the 90s. We've created a platform to deliver energy and daily inspiration as fuel to fight the spiritual war against demonic forces like abortion and LGBTQ equality. Plus, it is sponsored by our family osteria that I'm expanding into Rome." Pietro held up a flyer for his new restaurant.

Impressed by the man's business sense, Tommaso felt a twinge of optimism.

"And," Pietro said, "although the Cardinal is not with us today, he is sending messages for us to use on the podcast. He's encouraging the faithful to show up at the abortionist Trota's funeral. That can be a way to support the truth that the wages of sin are suffering and death.

Roger stood. "Indeed, my friends. The whole world is suffering and dying. The worst is in my own USA. The other day, President Joe Biden lit up the White House for what he called Pride month, lit up the building in rainbow colors. He said, and I quote, 'Today, the People's House sends a clear message to the country and to the world, 'America is a nation of pride'."

Roger paced back and forth at his end of the table. "But, America is a nation of shame, not pride. There and here, too, we're flirting with a destiny that destroys nations. The problem is getting worse as we hear politicians like Ellie Schlein say, 'I am a woman. I love another woman. I am not a mother, but I am not less of a woman for this.' But, women loving women do not populate countries. Mussolini was right: All nations first feel decadence gnawing at them when their birth rate falls off like Italy's has. It applies to the Holy Church, don't you see?"

Pietro nodded. "It's true that some social media

sites say the US is under 'demonic possession' at the hands of an ancient goddess of 'sexual immorality,' in a spiritual war. I've seen a claim that Satan himself is behind the LGBTQ rights movement. But better to overcome evil with good like our podcast is doing. We need to be patient in this work to save our sisters, our mothers and our daughters."

Tommaso cleared his throat. "Patience and love are good, Pietro, but we are running out of time."

Frank said, "Consider lesbians as witches, Father, who have got to be stopped from spreading their evil as if it is good. We see them entice and allure innocent others to increase in numbers, as they have done for centuries." He caressed the *Malleus* with his fingertips as if it were a talisman. "I suggest we create a success story to market, run it on Pietro's podcast." He nodded at Pietro.

"We take a nubile American Catholic, flaunting her sinful choice like the one I met on campus, just yesterday." Frank stood and circled the long table, his arms out in front of him as if carrying her. "We escort her to Vito's competent hands."

Roger exhaled loudly. "You mean you have a young woman in mind?"

"The perfect one for our purposes." Frank sat down and patted the *Malleus*. "As an enthusiastic young lesbian, she is headed for a future to indulge in every kind of carnal lust and all manner of filthy delights. We will give her a chance to repent, so she can be received back into the bosom of the Church.

We can videotape the process and share the dramatic transformation over Pietro's platform."

Tommaso said, "I pray God sends this young woman the 'grace of conversion' under Vito's compassionate and experienced tactics, perhaps even paired with obtaining Fredericka's grace of confession."

"You can trust me," Frank said. "I'll contact Xavier and Albert, assist them with a plan to pick her up this coming Friday evening. I know where she plans to be."

Pietro nodded. "That miracle would fit in with our plan for the podcast to send silent witnesses to a gay wedding, open to the public in an abandoned monastery. It will serve as a wake-up example of how far we have strayed from a faithful man and woman becoming one and replenishing the earth," said Pietro with a smile, closing his laptop and sliding it into a quilted case. "Please be my guest with a meal in the private dining room upstairs."

Even though he had no appetite, Tommaso felt nourished by the outcome of today's meeting.

27
HILLARY

At the front desk, Hillary introduced herself to a nun she hadn't met before and learned she was Sister Prudence. Hillary asked if there was any news about Fredericka.

"The Pope is calling for prayers." Prudence made the sign of the cross over herself.

"Of course," murmured Hillary. "I'm sorry to bother, but I need help renting a car. We have a couple places to go, and it takes so long waiting in lines at taxi stands to get back to the convent. I have an International Driving Permit."

"Certainly, and a space in a car park close by." The nun turned to type into the computer. "Give me a few minutes."

Hillary found the VW Passat a snap to operate, with its built-in GPS. She dropped Ed off at the

Marriott for their all-day program, and Claire got into the front seat. "We're early for basketball camp, Mom. Let's hit some of those Roman bookstores."

"Sure. Got any in mind?'

Claire grinned. "I found one, called Tuba's." She poked the address into the GPS on the dashboard.

As Hillary drove, Claire read from her phone: "Here's what the website says. 'Tuba is a lesbian-owned bookshop, bar and feminist space. It is a chill yet joyful place to get a drink and a bite to eat—especially for self-dubbed social justice warriors where you'll find not only books but also women writers to chat with.' 'Social justice warriors,' Mom! So cool!"

Hillary laughed. "Warriors on vacation. No one to battle here, right?"

"Just don't embarrass me with any weird comments about baby Jesus."

"I don't know where that came from, it just popped out!" Hillary shook her head.

She threaded through light traffic until she found the Pigneto neighborhood and a parking place nearby. Strolling along the pedestrian street, they pointed out to each other the rainbow flags flapping from store signs and on items in the windows.

Tuba's was packed with books, but mostly in Italian. After browsing the shelves for half an hour, Hillary bought a magazine and an English edition of Anna Maria Ortese's short story collection *Evening Descends Upon the Hills*. Claire purchased *Immodest Acts: The Life of a Lesbian Nun in Renaissance Italy*.

They sat to eat an early lunch, looking around the room and guessing which women might be the writers the website noted. They took turns looking at the magazine that had a photo of the missing Fredericka on the cover. A related article described a year-old kidnapping case, showing a photo of a young man being pushed into a small blue car. The piece was in Italian, but the word Mafia made the meaning clear. Despite the heat of the day, the blood in Hillary's arms ran cold.

She got up and led the way back to her rented car. She looked at Claire with narrowed eyes. "Never go anywhere with strangers, promise me," she said.

"Have more faith in how you raised me. I'm still here all in one piece, yes?"

Hillary nodded. "Yes. And keep it that way."

At the Global Sports Summer Camp, Hillary waited as Claire checked herself in at the registration table. Then Claire hauled her gym bag full of various colored uniforms and her mid-top Nike sneakers into the locker room.

Hillary found a seat in the gym bleachers and watched the young athletes scrimmage, impressed with the basketball IQ she saw displayed on the court.

At the reception after the game, she joined in getting to know others despite their diverse languages. She overheard Claire explaining to some giggling tweens how basketball worked in the WNBA. Hillary flushed with pride over her savvy young daughter.

28
HILLARY

The next day, Hillary dropped Claire off for her all-day basketball session and drove to the conference hotel while Ed fiddled with his laptop in the passenger seat.

"Should I create a Roman holiday for myself, or can I join you Polizia?" she asked.

Ed laughed. "Polizia. You're good, Genevieve. I told some of them how you've tripped up the bad guys a few times, yourself. They're glad to have you sit in as we start our group project."

Hillary turned into the hotel parking entrance. "What's on the agenda?"

"Yesterday, a session zeroed in on new digital tools. My group decided to try some today and dive into the deep web, investigate the recent kidnappings of the two women." She parked, he slid his MacBook Pro into his briefcase, and they made their way to the elevator.

As they waited, Hillary frowned. "I've heard of the dark web but not the deep web. It sounds like a setting in a gothic novel. Is it even real?"

"You use the internet with Chrome, right?"

"Safari."

"Okay, any browser keeps track of you with your IP address, like a return address on a letter. When you get to a website or send email, your IP address is attached, it shows where you are on the planet."

The elevator doors slid open, and they stepped in. "What floor?" she asked.

"Five."

She hit the button. "My IP gives our street address?"

"No, but it shows your city or at least your zip code. Your IP changes when you travel. You can check it out at 'what is my ip address dot com'."

"That's horrible and wonderful at the same time," she said.

"But if you are on the dark web, you can be anonymous. Users can hide their IP address with encryption that converts data into a hidden code. Banks and other places depend on it, of course. But bad guys adore it."

Hillary frowned. "Sounds like something from a conspiracy theory," she said.

"Good way to put it. We work down in bottom feeder land." He patted his briefcase. "Have to make sure we don't pick up any Trojan horses or other malware."

The elevator stopped. A stocky, bald man stepped in, elbowed Ed in the ribs and gave him a big smile.

"Hey, Genevieve," Ed said, "meet Billy, from Texas. He'll be running the show today." Hillary shook hands with Billy, feeling as if she'd known him a long time. At the fifth floor, Billy rushed off, saying he had to get the room arranged.

Ed took his time getting down the hallway. "We use custom software," he said, "to get into browsers that have encrypted entries. That's how we search the dark web to find postings from users talking, blogging and sharing files in secret."

Hillary knew this sort of thing went on, but she'd never paid attention to the details. She nodded for Ed to continue.

"Cybersecurity firms like Cisco and Okta share their findings even with little companies like mine, in Sacramento," he said.

"You never told me how worried I should be." Hillary's eyes narrowed.

He sighed. "Bottom line, the deep net is not searchable by web crawlers, but it's not necessarily evil. Some people just want reliable privacy, even families or friends. But most of the deep net is taken up by big organizations run by powerful men."

"When you get started today, I'll tuck myself in a corner, listen and learn," she said. Seeing how these law enforcement professionals work might calm her fears for Claire's safety.

In the meeting room, Ed introduced Hillary to a

petite woman, dressed in a navy-blue suit. It struck Hillary how much she looked like Rachel Maddow.

"Meet Sofia, aka Detective Rossi, or as she is formally known,'Investigatrice'." Ed gave a ta-da motion with his hand. "Her partner Mario says she outperformed her male colleagues and made it to detective."

Sofia tossed her head. "Our machismo is stronger than anywhere else on the planet." She stuck out her hand for a shake.

"Sofia worked a kidnap case here last year, a young man was shoved into a car and vanished," Ed said.

"I think I saw something about that in an article," Hillary said. "Related to the Mafia, yes?"

Sofia nodded. "It's still under investigation. Kidnap cases are my specialty. Aldo Roma was my uncle. You have heard of him?"

Ed nodded, but Hillary shook her head. "No, I'm sorry."

Sofia said, "He was kidnapped and killed, left on the sidewalk right in the middle of Rome, like a sack of potatoes. *Orribile*!"

She dabbed at her eyes with a white handkerchief. Hillary liked her immediately.

"His story is told in a fantastic tour of Rome. I recommend it for tourists if they have time," Sofia said, pocketing the handkerchief and squaring her shoulders.

While they talked, a half dozen others came in,

lanyards announcing their names and professional affiliations, some from private industry, others from government organizations. Some helped themselves to pastries and coffee, talking quietly among themselves. Hillary took a bear claw and drew a cup of French Roast for herself before she selected a place near the back of the room.

Others took their water bottles right away without pastry or coffee and settled into seats around the conference table in the middle of the brightly lit room with white boards on three sides.

The stocky, bald man Hillary had met in the elevator stood at the front. He called out, "Welcome, EuroUS team. Five minutes, and we get going."

He needed no mic. He turned and wrote at the top of the white board behind him: *Locate the kidnappers.*

Under that, he drew a line. Then he ran the black marker down the middle to create two columns. The right one he headed: *Fredericka, activist nun.* He headed the left column: *Trota, dead midwife.*

He looked at the group, seated at the white rectangle of conference tables butted up against each other. "Let's fill these columns with facts." He tapped on the right-hand column. "Make this more than a team building project. Make it real." He paused. "Find the missin' sista."

Hillary appreciated the way Billy's Texas twang dramatized the challenge of rescuing the nun.

Sofia walked to the front and picked up a marker.

She stood beside the Fredericka case column. “What are the connections? Keep in mind resemblances to previous abductions.”

“Both are women,” Ed called out. “Both related to controversial issues: one on abortion, the other, ordaining women priests.”

Another participant shouted, “Both Catholics. Both missing in Rome near tourist sites.”

“Only one is dead and tattooed, identified as a midwife who helped women get abortions. She supported that as a right by passing out flyers. Her funeral near the Roman pyramid is being publicized.”

“The other one marched in public with signs in favor of ordaining women priests. Her whereabouts are unknown.”

“Acts against women like these could be dreamed up by men frustrated over how the mainstream is headed,” said a man with an untrimmed beard sitting near Hillary in the back of the room. “Maybe some kind of religious zealots?”

A slim young man called out: “Backlash against progressives is snowballing, kidnapping may be used to get attention and political support. We could call it a deviant subculture.”

Someone else said, “Reminds me of the conference session yesterday outlining the four horsemen of terrorism—Nationalism, Socialism, Religious Extremism, Social Exclusion. Might sound too extreme for these cases?”

Hillary closed her eyes in the silence as members of the group seemed to be pondering the ideas.

Billy moved over to the blank white board on another wall. "How can we go online today and use our tech tools," he drawled. "Jean, what do you have to say?" He nodded at a man with an untrimmed beard sitting near Hillary.

Jean stood and spread open his arms in the shape of a living cross. "The online manosphere covers a spectrum—most incel forum posts look extreme. My gut tells me breaking into those could be useful."

Billy wrote "incel forums" on the white board. "Mario, what's cooking in that brain of yours?"

"The Trota and nun cases point to religious extremism, folks on the fringe, small but not that different from Jonestown or the Moonies, true believers we can hunt with our hacking tools," Mario said. Sofia nodded and sat down next to him.

Hillary was impressed by Mario's global references. The man knew how to build energy in the room. She noticed Ed had one eye on the conversation and the other on his laptop. He pointed to his laptop screen and said, "The '*Daily Bread*' podcast is urging people to attend Trota's funeral. But that won't be shown online, will it?"

"Trota's family has set up a service in the Protestant cemetery," Jean explained. "I don't think the funeral will be online, but digital tools could be useful to analyze the ink she was tattooed with."

Billy said, "Let's set the ink aside for now and nail

down who's producing that podcast. Could the Mafia have taken to the digital universe? And I suggest we focus on the living we can do something about. Where in the world might the missing nun be?"

"I know it might sound wild, but what about in a place like that abandoned monastery I heard about in the news last week, maybe one far away?" asked Ed.

Mario let out a whoop. "We've got hundreds, maybe thousands of abandoned monasteries in this country. I'm up for a needle in the haystack search for tiny villages and abandoned monasteries."

Ed remarked, "I found a Wildchan image-board site, but I can't get in yet. Could there be some kind of connection to the digital incel hate activity heating up?"

Sofia looked over at Ed. "I'm interested in learning how to get in to dark web forums," she said, "although we don't think the Mafia uses them yet, just face to face still, like the Red Brigade when they killed Uncle Aldo."

Ed nodded as he kept up his search. Hillary watched the room fall into silence as the tapping of keyboards replaced voices, all on the hunt for clues.

A COUPLE HOURS LATER, BILLY WALKED TO THE FRONT of the room. "It's been a productive session. Let's keep in touch about what we learn. It's time for lunch now before the afternoon sessions."

Ed looked up, a dazed expression on his face as Billy continued addressing the small group.

"You and your families are welcome to join us later for dinner at Pascals' Osteria. I've reserved a room for a dozen of us, but there is wiggle room. Before we break up, let's think about these cases as if we're writing a true crime TV show. Who would be the next victim? What would that tell us about the kidnappers?"

Hillary watched people pursing their lips and looking around at each other. Mario cleared his throat and stood. "I hate to say it but," he sighed, "could be a young woman, maybe gay, maybe a foreigner. Get maximum BBC attention."

Hillary gasped.

"But I'll be glad to be wrong," said Mario. "Let's find these crazies before they nab anyone else."

29
HILLARY

At dinner, Hillary pressed her Aperol Spritzer to one cheek then the other, combatting the heat of the evening as she listened to Claire describe basketball camp.

"Many of the kids are at the awkward age, running around the court, getting tangled up. You can see some of them confused over what is going on, not sure about their feelings. I'm excited I might see them when I come back next year for college."

Jean smiled at Claire. "Let me say, as a Frenchman raised in Rome, be careful when you're out on the town here. Don't get involved in anything political like a march or demonstration."

"Sister Fredericka made herself public," said Sofia. "She is a crusader, a brave woman, but yes, especially for tourists, it is best to keep a low profile."

"She stood up for what's right," said Claire.

"I'm only saying, pay attention to your surroundings and belongings," Jean said and refilled his wine glass.

"I do pay attention! But you're all paranoid, like my Dad." Claire blew Ed a kiss.

"Guilty as charged," Jean said, "but if God forbid, you are ever abducted, there are ways to increase your odds of survival. You don't want to be boisterous and, you know, yelling expletives," he said. "What you call it in America?"

Claire nodded. "Swearing."

"You want to be non-threatening, compliant—yet aware—of what's going on."

With one hand, Billy held his pizza high, letting the cheese string out, with the other, he raised his grappa-laced coffee. "Folks who get hurt," he said, setting down both his pizza and his coffee cup. He held his hands out far apart. "They'll be the loud mouths." He looked at Claire.

"Why are you all talking to me?" Claire asked. "I know how to watch out."

Hillary said, "Can't hurt to think about being careful. Maybe wear a jacket when you're out."

Claire looked down at her rainbow It's Cool to Be Kind tank top. "My Queer friends say I dress conservative."

Billy shook his head, downed the last of his spiked coffee, and ran his hands over his bald head. Hillary said to him, "I can't get used to that word either."

Claire scowled. "The word 'Queer' is inclusive. That's why I like it, and you should, too, Mom." She lifted her tank top straps with her thumbs. "I dress mostly in tee shirts though not after basketball this afternoon!" She laughed and patted the tattoo on her shoulder, a tiny Monarch butterfly topping an orange-and-tan basketball. "Had to show the kids the WNBA basketball."

"Well," drawled Billy. "You take care, young lady. If anything happens, memorize every detail: moles, piercings, scars, tattoos, anything that can help identify criminals." He got up to pay the check.

Identify criminals, thought Hillary. Thank God, no one had mentioned Mario's prediction of the next victim to expect. Or maybe it would have been better to warn Claire that way.

30
HILLARY

The next morning, Hillary woke to the sound of Claire arguing with Ed. "Dad, I'll be fine. They know their way around. They aren't kids. Jason is a professor, it's his birthday today, plus the end of the summer session!"

Hillary bolted upright. "Surely they wouldn't mind us coming along. I always celebrate back home when the semester is over. You know that, Claire." Hillary looked at Ed.

He squinched up his face and got a laugh out of Claire. "We're cool parents, right?" he said. "We won't embarrass you."

She shook her head. "Look at Mom's reaction to Jason's paintings! Over the top. You two go have a romantic dinner, and come pick me up later. I'll text when we're done."

"What time will that be?" Ed asked.

"Around 10:00, maybe."

"How about," Hillary said, "we'll drop you off where you're meeting them."

"Kids my age travel all over Europe on their own, Mom. Jason's picking me up. I'll be fine."

Fear seized Hillary. She had to be near where Claire would be hanging out with the students. "Where will he be taking you?"

"It's some pizza place in the Travestere, near the college. Violet told you that's a safe district."

"What is Jason's number?"

"Mom, you have Violet's number. How many numbers do you need?"

"What's wrong with caring about where you are?"

"You just care about showing you're the best mother ever. Smothering me has nothing to do with being a good mother. I'm going downstairs on my own to the breakfast room, now." She walked out and shut the door behind her.

Ed shook his head. "We are going to have to trust her. She's giving us no choice."

Hillary's shoulders slumped. A lump formed in her throat. She plugged her phone into the charger. Tonight would be no time to miss a text from Claire.

31
XAVIER

Xavier relaxed against the Lancia's leather passenger seat, listening to the investment tips from the radio, calculating the potential financial benefits.

Albert seemed fidgety, smoking a lot, as he headed for Rome. It was the third time for them. Why was Albert nervous?

When they left Wild Vines, the nun hadn't been giving Vito any trouble. She seemed in a trance, listening to him talk in his low, slow voice.

A few hours later, as they neared the ring road circling Rome, Albert stabbed out another Marlboro in the overflowing ash tray. He lowered the window and flipped the butt out. "Where's this dude Frank live?" he asked.

"Tommaso said text him for his address when we get near the Coliseum," Xavier said.

"What's the story on how Frank knows where to find the girl?"

"We'll ask when we pick him up. He'll be standing in front of an apartment building. You want me to put it into the GPS?"

"Yeah, go ahead. That's the queer district. I know the general direction but get the address up."

32
HILLARY

Hillary and Ed sat outside at Mimi e Coco's, in the Travestere neighborhood, near where Hillary guessed the pizza place might be. Hillary ordered a Campari Negroni. Ed asked for a Moretti craft beer along with Bruschetta to share.

She told Ed what Pauline had whispered after morning prayer in the chapel. "Guilty. She feels guilty that Sister Fredericka is missing. She encouraged Fredericka's activism."

Hillary's nerves danced with guilt over not stopping Claire from going with Jason for the pizza party. Guilt. Things done and not done. Such a risk. "It reminds me of when I used lines from other reporters. That guilt weighed me down for years. I imagined the shame my father would have felt if he'd found out. I still feel heavy in my arms and chest." She held her chin. "Even in my jaw."

Ed nodded. “But the university never penalized you, they even forgave you. It was just one sentence. And you apologized later. Your terrific Mea Culpa, they ran it in the student paper.” He refilled her glass with the Chianti Classico the server had recommended. “That sin still bothers you?”

“Yes. It does,” she said, “in a thin and watery way since my confession was published, sort of like the way this Chianti is different from our old vines Lodi zinfandel.” She swirled the wine in her glass. “How could Chianti really have been the wine Hannibal Lector served along with those fava beans!”

Ed laughed. “What a memory you have, Genevieve. And ways to change the subject!”

She swirled it again and pointed to the glass. “See, the Chianti leaves no legs, it’s thin. Not like me.”

“I love your legs.” Ed reached under the table to run his hand along her thigh. She laughed and set her glass down.

A whisper of tobacco floated by from the pipe of an old man sitting two tables away. Ed inhaled deeply. “Our Lodi wines,” he said. “I miss them like I miss those little cigars, my guilty pleasures from so long ago.”

Hillary picked up a dried cherry from the bowl on the table and tapped the tiny red fruit against the menu. “I’m ordering a huge Florentine steak as my guilty pleasure for tonight. Will you share a high calorie Bistecca with me as a stand in for a little cigar?”

33
XAVIER

Albert drove to where they saw a man of Frank's description standing by an old fountain with water pouring from a gargoyle built into the wall. Albert pulled over to the curb, and Frank let himself into the back seat.

"So, where we off to?" Albert looked over his shoulder.

"Pizza de Zizza. Travestere. The chef's from Napoli, home of the true Italian pizza," Frank said.

Albert raised a fist. "A tasty place. Picked up my share of Stacies in that part of town. But sounds straight, Frank. Why there to pick up a lesbian?" he asked.

"I keep tabs on the college LGBTQ community. Pizza de Zizza's where they hold their end of summer session party. What about your part? How you getting this lost soul into your car?"

Albert grunted.

Xavier laughed. "Albert plans to show how good he is at his game, get a lesbian to go with him."

"Good at his game?"

"He's a pickup artist. Got lots of lines for the ladies."

Albert blew a smoke ring. "I might sidle up to her and murmur I have hot Italian women asking me to hook them up with young American women. She could be interested in a fling over here in romantic Italy."

"Clever," said Frank. Xavier lowered his window, letting out smoke.

Albert carried on. "Or I might build intimacy, disclose personal details of being bisexual and knowing what lesbians like. Ask her what she likes, too."

"Creative."

"Or tell her my little sister wants out of the closet to our parents, but she's afraid. Needs someone who's been there to help her." He blew a double smoke ring toward the windshield.

"Got it," said Frank. "You are an artist, indeed." Xavier pegged Frank as not very savvy about the incel community.

Xavier explained the online forums and showed him on his phone.

Frank said, "I'm impressed with how you work together."

Xavier said, "Albert is practiced at picking up women, but not me. Even though it hurts, I'm about to give up the hunt. To face it. No one ever wanted me."

"Give it time," said Albert.

"Stupid of me to think I could get any of them to say yes. Hunting for love is about over now. But I still like to look."

Xavier eyeballed the putas who flaunted their half-naked bodies in the roadway, dressed in strips of silver and shiny red polyester, sexy females who would never give him a chance. Unless he paid them. He basked for a moment in his desire, and at the same time, fueled his anger.

Albert stubbed out another Marlboro, stuffing the butt down into the overflowing ashtray. He wound through the narrow streets, following Frank's directions to the pizzeria where the Queer Alliance was celebrating.

Frank said, "Okay, slow down. See the guy with the green beret and the turquoise hair? He's Jason, the club sponsor. Tell him Frank sent you to find out about the art history program. Say Xavier wants to go back to college and wants to make some LGBT friends. It's that little bitch with the big boobs covered with rainbows. Our perfect candidate."

"And a looker, too," said Xavier.

"You're supposed to be gay, kid. I'll get out on the next block."

Albert pulled over and let Frank out of the Lancia then circled back and parked near a gelato shop across the street in the next block, diagonal from Pizza di Zizza.

Xavier bought a scoop of pineapple gelato and joined Albert, seated outside the shop. Albert narrowed his eyes and peered at Claire, seated with a half dozen students at the table with Jason. "That girl. Not yet banged by a real man."

Xavier nodded, feeling glum. "How can we get her away from the others?" He dug into his gelato.

Albert lit another Marlboro, fiddled with the ash tray, and crushed the empty red box.

Xavier's face flushed. "How to get her to go with us?" He studied the students.

Albert said, "That green beret guy's tall but scrawny. She looks pretty fit, does some kind of martial art, plays a sport. Let's go get to know them. At some point, I'll give her my sob story about my little sister, Maria."

AFTER ALBERT INTRODUCED THEM AS FRANK'S FRIENDS, Jason invited them to join their table. Albert took a few sips of beer and a bite of pizza then began working his magic. It didn't take him long to get Claire's attention.

Xavier admired the way Albert choked up and became close to tears as he spun his story. "Maria's afraid to tell our parents. She been… cutting herself."

"I did that too! It was awful. She has to know it will get better," Claire said.

Albert frowned. "I've been saying that!"

"There's help out there," Claire said, and a couple other students nodded agreement.

"I've been telling her that, but… she ignores me." Albert's shoulders slumped.

Xavier mirrored Albert's frown and murmured, "It's tragic."

Claire gave a bright smile. "Most parents are cool and support their kids."

Albert stared at her. "She's afraid she'll be disowned. Or worse. Her friend Lucinda was attacked while getting into her girlfriend's car. Her father grabbed her by the hair and slapped her, while her mother called her Liella. She's afraid our parents will beat her. I think they would, too."

"My mom and dad surprised me with how great they were."

Albert sighed. "She might…maybe she would believe it, coming from you. Can you come talk to her?"

Claire wrinkled her nose and shook her head.

"I'm so worried." Albert held out his phone and showed her a photo. "She used a butcher knife this time."

Claire let out a low whistle. "Why ask me? Doesn't she have any girlfriends?"

"They're like rabbits, scared of their own shadows. You're so strong. Look what a good time you're having, out here and happy. She's down the street, drowning her sorrows in gelato. Just come talk to her for a few minutes. Please."

She blew out a long, soundless breath. "I've got to go to the toilet," she said to Jason. He nodded.

Xavier watched Claire walk away from the others.

XAVIER OPENED THE LANCIA'S BACK DOOR AND SLID onto into the seat behind Claire. In the dim light, he glanced down. The new silk scarves were in place next to the baggie, and a neoprene bungee cord sat coiled on the seat beside him, just in case.

The car pulled away from the curb. Lucky there was no traffic.

"What's Maria's number?" Claire asked. "I'll text I'm coming to talk to her."

"I'll put it in for you." Albert stretched out his hand.

Xavier held his breath.

She gave him her phone.

Albert looked down at its face and tossed it over his shoulder into the back seat.

"Stop!" Claire screamed. "What are you doing! Let me out!"

Stretching the ends of the scarf into a silky rope, Xavier reached the fabric over and slid it between her lips, then tied it into a knot at the back of her head.

Claire grunted and kicked at the door

Xavier could see Albert's lips stretched back in a grin. She was a noisy one, howling from under the silk and scraping her nails against the Lancia's leather seat.

Xavier'd hoped she would be cool. He lowered his window a few inches, lifted the damp cloth out of the baggie, and reached around to press it under Claire's nose.

Albert was a genius with this mixture. A genius.

She quieted. Nothing but a faint hum from deep in her throat.

Albert tuned the radio to the business station. There it was again. How to get rich. Attract the woman of your dreams.

Xavier daydreamed about a heart tattoo, with a woman's name in the middle. Maybe just the words "My Darling" would look good. He smiled at his fantasy. If only he had the pickup artist skills of Albert.

34
HILLARY

Hillary picked up her spoon and pushed the chocolate gelato around in its little bowl. She couldn't make herself take a bite. Her insides quivered. Claire hadn't texted. Hillary would never forgive herself if anything happened to Claire.

She snuck a look at her phone and waited until five past ten before she said, "Nothing from Claire yet."

Ed said, "I'm concerned, but we can wait some, everything runs late here." He was nearly done with his cannoli.

The waiter came by and gave her a quizzical look. She leaned back and let him clear away her unfinished dessert. "We don't even know the name of the place! I'm calling Violet."

"Claire will be furious."

"I'll text instead, ask her to not let on to Claire."

Hillary poked in a text to Violet and waited, holding her breath. After a minute and no reply, she said, “Violet is not responding. I don’t have Jason’s number. I’m going to text Claire.”

Almost immediately, a Not Delivered message bounced back. She held up the phone for Ed to see. He frowned.

Hillary punched in Claire’s phone number. A mechanical voice announced, “This call cannot be completed.”

“Her phone is dead,” Hillary whispered. “Where is she?”

Ed pursed his lips and took out his phone.

Hillary clutched at her stomach and ran for the bathroom. Barely making it into a stall, she let go of her dinner. She stood gasping for a few seconds before she washed her flaming hot face and rinsed her mouth. She ran back to the table to see Ed on his phone, nodding as he listened.

He ended the call. “That was Violet. She didn’t answer you because she was in the shower. She said she wasn’t sure where they were going but gave me Jason’s number.” He thumbed the number.

“Hey, Jason. This is Ed, Claire’s dad. Happy birthday, man.”

The next minute felt like a year. Hillary hunched over and hugged herself tight as she listened.

“We’re wondering where to go pick her up if the party’s over?”

Hillary flung her hands into the air.

Ed nodded, then shook his head. "She never texted us. Her phone is dead. I'm going to call the police, Jason. They'll want to talk to you. When was the last time you saw her?"

More silence.

Ed ended the call. He stared at Hillary, shaking his head as he thumbed another number.

"Sofia. Ed here. Our daughter is missing."

Hillary clenched the table. "Our daughter is missing," she breathed, the blood in her veins standing still.

35
XAVIER

It was late when they got back. Albert parked in his usual spot. The night light in the apartment courtyard was the only illumination among shadows cast by the rooftops. Eleanora had long ago turned out the office lights.

Albert scooped up the unprotesting Claire from the front seat and lifted her out.

Xavier noticed her face looked like that picture of the sleeping princess in the book of fairy tales Father Joseph let him read when he was a good boy. Her lips were pale, parted around the gold silk scarf. Her blond hair clung to the sides of her cheeks in damp curls.

Albert carried her to the bench at the bottom of the trail. She wasn't making a sound. Was she all right? "Has she been out too long?" Xavier asked Albert.

"Nah. She's young. Tie her legs together and get her onto my back."

Xavier bound her at the knees and ankles with red scarves. Albert knelt on the path for Xavier to hoist her into piggyback position, her arms over Albert's shoulders.

ONCE THEY GOT DOWN INTO THE LIGHTED WORKSPACE, they found Vito dozing in the camp chair. He jumped up and said, "Sister Fredericka's still out cold. Good inhalants you make, Albert. Just a whiff relaxed me. You should get into the designer drug business. Make a pot of money."

"Got uppers, too, bring you out from downers," Albert said. He jerked his chin in the direction of the shelf.

Vito nodded. "I bet you do." He put on his jacket. "I'm staying in a room in the village. See you tomorrow."

Xavier freed Claire off Albert's back. They laid her out in the niche they'd prepared for her, next to Fredericka's.

Albert sank to the floor and crawled into his sleeping bag.

Xavier pulled up the white top sheet to just under Claire's chin. She lay still, breathing in and out with a half-smile on her lips. He ran his fingertips up and down the side of her cheek. She was safe here.

Exhausted, Xavier crawled into his sleeping bag next to Albert's. Albert was snoring.

Xavier was still wired and had to tell himself the story of Sleeping Beauty a few times before he felt himself drifting off.

36
HILLARY

Hillary sat in Claire's alcove, on her bed, cradling her daughter's pillow, caressing it as if it were a baby. "I should never have let her go! I should have planted my body in her way." She breathed in Claire's scent from the pillow.

Ed was hip by hip beside her, rubbing her back. "You know how strong willed she is. Neither of us could have stopped her."

She turned to him, a wadded white hanky clutched in her hand. "She might be all alone, abandoned." She searched the face of this man she loved, his eyes now a dark turquoise.

A knock sounded its way into the suite. "That must be Sofia." Ed answered the door.

At attention stood a tall, uniformed officer next to Sofia. Mario.

A thread of tension drained from Hillary's shoulders. Here was that petite detective, in a navy-blue suit, jacket buttoned over an open collar white blouse, on the job after midnight.

And Mario with her. Hillary felt the comfort of order.

"Come sta? How are you doing?" Sofia said without waiting for an answer. "The department has put Claire's face on the national police system and sent out an all-points bulletin. We have a few questions. May we come in?"

"Of course." Ed waved them into the suite.

Feeling numb, Hillary stood, clutching Claire's pillow to her chest and reached out to hug Sofia, nearly knocking her over.

"What can we do?" Hillary heard herself, almost begging.

"Sit down before you fall down. Please." Sofia waited for Hillary to sit back down. "We are considering this an abduction in progress and working with the FBI through your embassy. We've set up checkpoints on the ring road out of Rome using the photo of her you sent over your phone."

Ed said, "The FBI works from the embassy? I thought they operated through Europol 24/7. Listen to me." He slapped his palm against his forehead. "Never mind. We need all the help we can get."

Sofia nodded. "International cases mostly fall into criminals seeking ransom or terrorist organizations like al Qaeda and ISIL making demands. But the abduction of your daughter fits what we predicted Tuesday." She looked at Ed with a grimace on her face. "I am sorry we were so right on."

He nodded with a clenched jaw.

"In its *orrible* way, it is better than a random kidnapping that leads to a dead-end. Here, we see a pattern."

"You're working to find the missing nun, yes? I've seen you here in the convent. Sister Pauline told me you questioned Mother Catherine. You and Mario," she nodded at him.

"Yes, and now we have notified the Office of Children's Issues at the American State Department."

Hillary twisted her white hanky into a thin rope. *Claire would hate hearing she is considered a child.*

"This is Saturday, so more challenge, but we are doing everything we can to rescue her," said Sofia, her bright brown eyes afire with intention.

"Rescue her," said Hillary through clenched teeth, pressing her Mary medal so tight her fingertips were white.

Sofia said, "I hate to ask, but is it possible Claire could have left on her own?"

Hillary froze. Ed's jaw dropped. "No. I'm sure she would not have run off. Certain."

Sofia nodded. "Yes, I just had to ask. These investigations go faster now since Netflix on the teen missing long ago. You saw?"

Hillary shuddered. That documentary. "Vatican Girl." The mystery of Emanuela Orlandi's disappearance. "She's never been found?"

Sofia shook her head and pulled a notepad out from an inside jacket pocket. "Where did you last see your daughter?"

Hillary ignored the traces of chocolate gelato talking back to her from her belly. "It was here, at the front desk. She was leaving to get picked up for a pizza party." She shook her head. "We were going out to dinner. We should have made her stay with us." She looked at Ed.

He sighed. "We were torn between overprotecting and giving her the independence she craved."

Sofia nodded, as she took notes. "So, what time was that?"

"Around 7:30. That was the last time we saw her," Hillary said, glaring at Sofia as if she were the kidnapper. "After that, nothing."

Sofia nodded and wrote a few more words, then closed her notebook. "That case I worked last year, the young man snatched from out in front of a restaurant, he was found out on the road the next morning."

"So, Claire could turn up in the morning." Hillary brightened.

"His case has some similarities, the age of the victims, and being taken from a restaurant as you think Claire was," Sofia said. "With him, though, witnesses calling for help right away let us get camera footage to identify the car which picked him up and headed full throttle towards the ring road."

Hillary was breathing fast, Claire's pillow pressed to her chest.

"We reached out to Violet for Jason Daniels address," Sofia continued, "got him out of bed and grilled him. Now at least we know the location of that pizza place but have to check out any cameras that might have caught anything."

"What did Jason say? He was supposed to keep his eye on Claire!" Hillary's throat felt clogged with guilt. She should have insisted on going for pizza with them, she, a professor in her own hometown! She should have spoken up.

Sofia reached out to rub Hillary's shoulder. "He said she was having a great time, fit right in with the college kids, and then went to the toilet. She never came back to the group. He texted her and phoned, but nothing was working. He feels awful and wants to do anything to help."

"What can he do?"

"Leave it to us," Sofia said. "The alert won't reach the public until morning. We asked for call in tips to help locate Fredericka and now Claire, over TV and all other media."

Hillary's stomach clenched as Sofia continued.

"There are major differences in the cases. The boy's father had been shot in the legs in May. The boy's kidnapping seemed linked to settling Mafia accounts. We have no sense that Claire's disappearance is connected to the Roman underworld." She looked at her partner Mario. "Unless there is something going on that's being kept from us." He pursed his lips tight.

In a quiet voice, he said, "Valeri's investigation is out of our hands now. It's with the anti-mafia magistrates of Rome." He nodded and Sofia stuck her notebook back into her pocket and turned to leave.

"Mario has been following a podcast from the traditional religious camp. He tells me they are urging people to attend the murdered midwife's funeral service. They claim that Trota suffered death for her sin of aborting Italian babies, shrinking the country rather than building it for what they call the glory of God."

Hillary shook her head and squeezed Claire's pillow tight to her belly. Ed was trembling with rage.

Sofia and Mario walked to the door. "Ed. Stand by. There might be some searching you can do on your laptop," said Mario. "Hillary, if you feel up to it, consider attending the midwife's memorial. Some criminals want to gloat over their successes. Go, scan the crowd for anyone looking smug and proud or such."

Mario opened the door and Sofia walked through ahead of him. She turned and said, "A presto. We will talk later." Mario gave a nod and closed the door behind them.

Hillary collapsed onto Claire's bed, clutching her stomach. Pain cradled her belly the way it had when she was ten and learned that her mother was gone. Her ears hummed and buzzed.

She looked over at the tidy alcove. The bed and closet there were supposed to have been for Paisley. Maybe she could come help, somehow. Should she text her? Paisley did love Claire.

No. This was not about her. This was her own darling daughter. She wrapped her arms in a tight hug then stood up.

"What's the matter with me? I've tracked down criminals before. I'm on the case now!"

She went to Ed, who was back on his computer. "You work with Sofia and Mario, use that new tech. I'll go to Trota's memorial. See if any kidnappers return to gloat."

37
XAVIER

Xavier woke, curious to see how Claire was doing this morning. Would she wake up on her own or need the anti-sedation drug? He pulled over a tall stool and sat watching Claire, sleeping on her back in the niche, bouncing her hands as if she was dreaming. He noticed the yellow scarf binding her wrists was the nearly same color as her hair.

He held his breath and touched her hair with his fingertips, drawing them around the curve of a loose curl. His breath came slowly and shallow. He reached down and loosened the silk scarf from around her wrists and pulled it towards him, letting her arms fall free. Was he imagining it or did she smell like lemons?

Albert poked his head into her niche. He started singing. Xavier never heard Albert sing. He was crooning something to Claire. Xavier made it out as "We love the split tails of the world."

The silk scarf muffled Claire's moans. Albert lifted her and pulled her out from the niche. He stood her up, her legs bound with the silk scarves from last night. "What's this?" His palms cupped her breasts and pressed her against the wall. "Your shirt, strutting Pride? Only talking about gay sex drew a fine in 15th century Italy. And you plaster you are queer across your breasts!"

Claire shoved his hands away. Albert gripped her wrists with one of his hands, and with the other, patted her breasts.

She started hopping, her legs tied together making her feet a battering ram.

"You mermaid!" Albert gripped her hips and slid her down the packed earth wall. She sat, grabbing for his legs, rocking and pounding her back against the wall, in rhythm to her muffled moans.

"Too bad you swallowed my gay sister line. It was nice you wanted to help her." Albert laughed.

She grunted and pulled at her silken gag.

"We can't have you taking off your golden scarf, now can we?" Albert pushed her hands down against her thighs. He retied the red scarves, binding her wrists to her knees.

"I like the feisty ones," he called out to Xavier. "Tell her what the *Malleus* says causes a woman to be queer?"

Before he knew it, a quote poured from Xavier's lips: "The devil can darken her understanding until she considers her husband so loathsome that not for all the world would she allow him to lie with her."

Claire grunted. "Ooo aaee!"

Albert crowed, "What's that? I'm crazy? He pulled down the neck of her shirt. "Oh, look what I found. How about I give you a free tattoo? Add a stinger to this butterfly on your shoulder!"

Claire's eyes opened wide. Guttural cries poured from deep in her throat.

Xavier was sweating. He heard Vito coming down the stairs. Now they could get serious.

Vito walked in and stood looking down at Claire. He frowned at Albert. "What a way to welcome our new guest, Albert. Let's calm down. It's time to get Sister Fredericka up, too. Xavier, post to the forum, and ask Father Tommaso to join us. We need to get the day's work started."

Xavier opened the laptop to start the message. His fingertips tingled as he typed, "Dear Father Tommaso, Vito is asking…" He shook his hands, finished the message without further sensations, and hit Send.

He turned to helping Vito get the two women settled. Fredericka went calmly to the other room and after ten minutes, she returned and took her seat like a noble woman. Xavier set a cup of herb tea by her.

They had to tie Claire into her chair.

---

she considers her husband so handsome that not for all the world would she allow him to be with her."

Claire groaned. [illegible]

Albert crowed. "What's that? [illegible]" [illegible] pulled down the neck of her shirt. [illegible]

[illegible]

Xavier was watching. He heard [illegible] coming down the stairs. [illegible]

[illegible]

Xavier [illegible] the laptop [illegible] message. His [illegible]

[illegible]

He turned to [illegible] the two women [illegible]

They had to find Claire [illegible] for them.

38
FATHER TOMMASO

Tommaso made his slow way down the stairs into the open lighted space. He stood, looking from one woman to the other as he addressed them. "You both have been deceived … by evil spirits. We are here to help you … return you to your true natures," he said, wheezing as he talked.

Claire shook her head back and forth, howling like a muzzled dog around the edges of her silk gag.

Fredericka listened.

Tommaso nodded, his hands crossed over his chest. "The One True Church guides and directs us in the ways of harmony according to the Father's Law."

He looked at Fredericka. "I hope you've reconsidered your position, Sister. Anyone who insists on promoting the idea of female ordination has left the foundation of the faith. Heresy carries with it your exclusion from the Church—excommunication."

Fredericka responded in a loud voice, "Times change. Last month, priests in Germany held blessing services for lovers, open to homosexual as well as heterosexual couples. Those blessings took place in eighty cities."

"Our Pope does not approve of that," shouted Tommaso.

Fredericka retorted, "Pope Francis has shown homosexuals not just tolerance but support, with five words: 'Who am I to judge?' And he defended legalizing same-sex civil unions."

Claire was grunting and flailing in her chair.

Tommaso turned to Xavier. "Get one of the little baggies. Sedate the young one lightly, so she can follow my work on Fredericka."

While Xavier did as instructed, Tommaso carried on. "Repent now, Sister, and return to God's grace, be a good example for the young Claire," he said. A cape of love for the nun fell over Tommaso as if she were a blood relative, one he'd not been blessed with in life. "Or be damned to everlasting hell."

He made the sign of the cross on Fredericka's brow. "I command you depart, unclean spirit, along with your minions now attacking the servant of God. Depart!"

Fredericka smiled. "No unclean spirit here, Father. Swallowing our anger is no longer an option. That's what the march was. Our voices, out loud."

She picked up her cup of tea. "Ciao," she toasted and drank down the entire contents.

A shaft of sunlight angled off to the side and winked out. The space darkened. Vito lit a couple oil lamps.

Tommaso kept up his censure, but Fredericka was silent for the next hour. "She's gone catatonic," Vito said.

"Dragged down by the devil." Tommaso looked at Vito. "I've got to rest. You work on the young woman, weaker in spirit."

39

HILLARY

Hillary had spent hours tossing and turning in bed. Once she fell asleep, she didn't wake until eleven. She struggled out from under the duvet and found Ed glued to his computer like a man possessed.

"Any word from Sofia?" she asked.

He shook his head. She peered over his shoulder. She couldn't tell what she was looking at. "What is that?"

He reached for her hand, rubbed it against the stubble on his cheeks, and kissed her palm. "I'm searching the manosphere for kidnap mentions. These are incel forums."

"What's happening?"

"Hate is happening, like it's women's fault these guys are still virgins, involuntarily celibate. Plenty of rape and hate talk but nothing on kidnaping."

Hillary sighed. Hate. That BBC article Ed showed

her on the plane was stamped into her brain. A slim figure in black threw the midwife's body into the Trevi.

A slim figure in black. What might the midwife's kidnappers look like? How crazy was it to think any of them would show up at her funeral. Was it possible they could be the same as those criminals who'd taken Fredericka and Claire?

She straightened. Stood tall. A steely hardness came over her, a sense of being on a hunt. She dressed quickly and left the convent, running over cobblestones to the car park, intent on getting to the funeral before noon. Maybe she could spot something. Someone.

She punched Protestant Cemetery into the GPS. Up popped the route to Cimitero Acattolico. Driving parallel to the ancient Roman Wall, she passed by the miniature pyramid, pulled into the crowded lot at ten before noon, and found one of the last open parking spaces.

She'd read somewhere that these graves were final resting places for non-Catholics and protestants—people who were not allowed Catholic burial. Centuries ago, services for the dead used to be held at night to avoid displays of religious fanatics.

Hillary checked the faces of the people holding signs. Fanatics. All around, people walked from cars holding signs, a few printed with "the wages of sin is death - Romans 6:23," some with ABORTIONIST in a circle, a diagonal line slashed through the word.

Other signs read "Give us this Day, a podcast for true believers."

She turned to gaze over a meadow lined with majestic cypresses. Tombstones dotted the dark green meadow. A few kittens scampered among the graves as if they owned the place. Hillary smiled at the frisky cats and let loose her shawl of anger for a moment.

Off to the left, near a wooden fence lined with foliage, she spotted the center of the sign-holders' attention. Under the shadow of a cypress tree stood two women. One held what looked like a small marble sculpture.

More sign-holders came tramping over the gravestones on the football-field-sized section of the cemetery. Near the fence stood a small table, holding a metal box. Next to the box was a photo of the slim young woman, Trota, her chestnut brown hair falling softly onto her shoulders.

Hillary stood a way off from the crowd and searched each face. Many looked masked with hate, but no one seemed clearly a suspect.

The woman holding the sculpture began speaking. "We are gathered to remember the life of a special volunteer in our party, Trota Mancini, a brave young woman, who helped the poor get health services they so needed. She was an honor student in the class of midwives from University of Rome Tor Vergata, some of whom are with us." She nodded and smiled at a half dozen young women next to the table. "Thank you for coming. Many of Trota's classmates have now migrated to other countries due to our economic difficulties and the problematic status of midwives here, with only half the new grads getting hired. Going by my Jewish tradition, I trust that all souls who reside in purity, as did Trota, return to God's eternal kingdom."

The woman next to her began speaking. "Grazia. My daughter was honored to work with Ellie Schlein's party to bring equality of services to all women in need. She helped so many women safely birth their babies, and they've come to express their sorrow at the horrible way she died." She reached out to hug a woman with a baby strapped onto her back.

"My great sorrow is that I disowned her for supporting legal abortion. And now it's too late." She wiped at her eyes. "She had been… violated..." Her chest heaved in silent sobs. "She never told me until last month that she had one when she was 13. It was her … Uncle!" She blew her nose and shook her head.

"Trota lives on in our memories now. She is in heaven, meeting with her father there. Here below her ashes will lie near his in his small family tomb. Trota is forgiven by our Lord, a God of mercy." She held the sculpture up high. "I leave on their grave Clementia, the goddess of forgiveness and mercy and clemency. May God forgive my daughter's rapist and her killers."

Jolts of anger shot though Hillary. *I can't forgive them.* They have my daughter. She was numb, suspended, no longer sensed her two feet planted on earth. She felt herself reaching, stretching, flying, darting, her eyes open and focused like a laser, red hot and zipping around to each face in the crowd.

Someone began singing the Lord's Prayer in Italian.

E rimetti a noi i nostri debiti. Forgive us our debts, our trespasses.

Come noi li rimettiamo ai nostri debitori. As we forgive our debtors, who trespass against us.

Forgiveness. Hillary thought of Sister Pauline and the Our Father in the chapel. Forgiveness.

No. First rescue, then revenge. Forgiveness was not Hillary's way.

She searched the crowd another time. Were the kidnappers here? Many of these sign-carriers looked like criminals, clasping their accusing signs.

Hillary stayed to pray at the midwife's graveside before she went back to the parking lot. Angela Narratrice, the BBC reporter, was there interviewing a sign-holder who was saying she supports life while she waved a "wages of sin is death " sign.

Hillary waited for the reporter to finish before she spoke up. "My daughter…" She could barely get the words out. "Was kidnapped."

"The American girl? We've got a story running on it," Angela said. "I'd love to get your statement."

Hillary nodded. "Claire was so excited to be here for basketball camp and tour the college she wants to go to. I beg anyone who saw anything near Pizza Zizza to contact the police right away!"

Hillary messaged a photo of Claire to Angela, who promised to update the story.

Back at the convent, Hillary called Sofia and told her going to the funeral was not useful except for getting Narratrice to include Hillary's plea in her BBC story.

As soon as she hung up from Sofia, Hillary got a call from Jason Daniels.

"I'm so sorry!" he said. "The police questioned me, and I told them everything I know, but I feel so guilty for getting distracted and letting Claire get away from the group. I know you must hate me."

Hillary couldn't tell who she hated anymore, there were so many.

She held her breath, her heart pounding, as Jason talked on in a rush. "I want to tell you what I saw. A tall blond man calling himself Antonio sidled up to Claire, said he was a friend of Frank's. That's my roommate, so I trusted the guy. He started giving Claire some kind of story about his sister, but..." Jason let out a loud sigh. "He probably didn't even have a sister. After a while, I noticed Claire fidgeting like she wanted to get away from him. She headed for the toilet. I figured she was safe there and got into a conversation with a guy running the emerging artists exhibit. When I noticed Claire wasn't back, I sent

Deborah to check, and Claire had disappeared. We asked all over the restaurant and went outside and checked even across the street, but she was gone. I'm so sorry!"

Hillary's chest was heaving and she could barely speak. "We're doing anything, everything to try and help the police find her," she said.

"I want to help, too. The only thing I can think of is to go to a gay wedding in case any demonstrators show up, maybe give a clue to the kidnappers."

Hillary's head buzzed. Going to a wedding wouldn't do any more good than going to that funeral had.

"The *Daily Bread* podcast is calling it shameful," Jason said. "They're inviting people to go protest the wedding of two women."

"No. I don't see how that could help us find Claire." Hillary hung up.

40
XAVIER

Claire was moaning. The inhalant had nearly worn off. Vito told Xavier to rewrap the scarves around Claire's knees, let her feet hang over the end of the lounge. Albert rubbed Claire's belly and cooed, "Have babies. Find out how happy you can be when you obey God's will."

"Leave her alone, Albert," Vito said. "Turn on the music."

Strains of "Clair de Lune" flowed into the open space. Its slow tempo made Xavier feel he was floating. He slapped his cheeks to bring himself back to the task of moving the Boxio sink into the open space, near Claire's feet. Earlier, he had heated water on the Coleman stove in the back room, trying to be quiet, not to disturb Father Tommaso, seated at the altar, praying.

Out in the open space, Xavier poured warm water

into the Boxio sink. Vito took a cup and dipped it into the water. He spilled it over Claire's feet and let it trickle into the sink as he spoke in a slow, soothing tone. "Allow your eyes to close. Take a deep breath in through your nose, and exhale slowly through your mouth."

Albert sat at his closed laptop, watching Vito.

In a slow cadence, Vito said, "Bring your attention to the sensations of your breathing. Notice the air moving in and out, the rise and fall of your belly. With each inhale, feel your body relaxing a little more. With each exhale, tension and stress melt away."

Xavier watched wide eyed, partly in fascination and partly to keep himself from falling into trance.

"Now shift your focus to your body. Scan from head to toe, noticing any areas of tightness or discomfort. As you bring your attention to each part, visualize that area softening and letting go."

Claire shook her head, her blond curls jiggling. Vito leaned near her face, and said, "Imagine a warm, soothing light at the top of your head. This golden light flows down, washing over your forehead, your eyes, your cheeks. Feel the tension dissolving as the light reaches your jaw and neck. The light continues down, reaching your shoulders."

Her shoulders twisted against the silk scarves, and she moaned. "Allow your shoulders to release any held-up stress. The light flows down your arms, to your hands and fingers, releasing any clenching or gripping."

Claire bent her arms at the elbows and wagged her fingers in the air.

"Bring your attention to your chest and belly. As you breathe, feel this area expanding and contracting gently. Let the light envelop this part of your body, allowing it to fully relax."

Xavier was amazed to see Claire following Vito's directions. Xavier got up and took a scarf off the table, thinking he might need to slip it between her lips if she started yelling.

"The soothing light now moves down to your hips, your thighs, your knees. Each area softens and lets go as the light washes over it. Reaching your calves, ankles, and feet, your entire body is now completely relaxed."

Claire took a deep breath.

"Take a few more deep breaths, savoring this state of profound relaxation. When you're ready, gently open your eyes, feeling calm, rested, and restored."

Claire opened her eyes and frowned. "You must be crazy."

Vito reached to massage her feet, and she yanked them away. "I'm not going along with this farce," she said.

"Claire," Fredericka said, "Listen to Vito, just listen, that's all." Claire narrowed her eyes.

Xavier found himself holding his breath. Claire needed to cooperate, save herself.

"Relax," Vito said, "Imagine you are a baby, surrounded by love. Both your mother and father love you. Remember how it felt to be loved by both of them. One a woman, one a man." Claire nodded.

"Love," Vito said. "Love surrounds you and God's love is all around us. We can choose to love in a way that brings us lasting joy, that brings us life."

Claire stared at Vito. Xavier got the sense that she was really hearing him. She closed her eyes as Vito talked on in a low drone. "At your body level, your response to erotic stimuli from women might seem more noticeable. But it might be that you also have noticed a response to young men from time to time."

Claire took a deep breath and exhaled loudly.

"But in your unconscious mind, you may have shut off that aspect of being attracted to someone." Vito put his hand on her shoulder and rubbed it in a small circle. "Then you have your beliefs and values, how you've been raised. You were confirmed in the Catholic Church that teaches how blessed it is to be in a sacramental marriage, open to life, to children."

Claire smiled.

Vito rubbed Claire's other shoulder. "All those aspects interact and play against each other. You have the power of personal choice, conscious choice, Claire."

"But consider the historical context," called out Fredericka. "How the church wants to be in control all the time. Maybe that is not true to who you are, Claire?"

Vito nodded to Albert. "Quiet the nun."

Albert grabbed a silk scarf and gagged Fredericka.

Claire began shaking her head back and forth and growling in the back of her throat.

"Can't stop up that voice of hers." Albert scowled.

She threw her legs high in the air, and bucked up and down, twisting and turning. Xavier watched, fascinated. Claire kept throwing her legs up and pounding them down until the lounge chair tipped and hung on one side for a moment then toppled over, pinning Claire beneath it.

Vito stood, his face dark with frustration, his jaw clenched.

"Superhuman strength is a sign of possession, it says in the *Malleus*," Xavier said. "The devil is battling to take control of her." He was stunned to hear those words coming from his mouth.

Vito wiped off sweat dripping from his forehead. "Go tell Father Tommaso we're going to need him to come do his part."

41
HILLARY

Ed reminded Hillary that Jean had asked them to go see him in his office near the Vatican. He might have come up with some new ideas on ways to look for Claire.

Hillary called Sofia, with a tingle of hope. Nothing new had turned up. Hillary's stomach twisted, her nerves twitched. All these days with Claire, her daughter struggling to be proud and independent, those hours and days felt like bliss compared to the agony she felt now.

Joy. It was so long ago. Where was Claire? Her baby. Her princess. Her only child. She had saved little blond seven-year-old Claire from being thrown off the top of Yates tower. She had stopped the bombing of the youth center, where petite twelve-year-old Claire could sharpen her point guard skills. Now she had to save her from whoever snatched her away. Who was that who'd stolen her joy? Maybe Jean could help them.

The Italian accent from the GPS directed Hillary to the business district south of the historic center on this bright morning. Its artificial cool voice had become an unexpected balm in the nightmare of Claire's disappearance. In the passenger seat, Ed worked away on his laptop.

Hillary parked in the underground lot. She and Ed took the elevator to the 8th floor and followed the hallway until they found the door lettered "Allied Europe Security."

Jean was waiting for them in the reception area. "Come on," he said. They followed him into his office.

Hillary was stunned by the view from the huge window behind his desk. There it was in all its finery: the Vatican, an enclave of beauty and riches, like an immense vault spread out on the west bank of the Tiber, topped by the ornate dome of the Basilica.

Her vision blurred. She blinked fast, shook her head, and looked at Ed. She could almost hear him thinking as he turned to her with his eyes wide. Still that shade of turquoise that turned her knees to Jello all those years back. Her whole body felt like Jello now, quivering. She waited for Ed to ask the obvious question.

"So? How does this help find Claire?" Ed asked.

Jean pursed his lips and scowled. He pointed to the Basilica. "I wanted you to get a feeling for the layered power of the church, of believers terrified they are losing control. For what's at stake. The kidnappings are just a small and public aspect of the battle going on underground."

He walked to a dictionary stand carved of walnut. "Last year, I wouldn't have noticed any of this. But six months ago, my wife left me—said I was killing her, trying to control her every move. I didn't think she meant it, but she died of heart failure last month. I've had weeks to reflect, time to look at memories from a new angle."

He let out a sigh. "Subtle violence against women isn't being done by monsters or aliens, it's being done by friends, neighbors, co-workers, clergy, fathers, brothers, uncles. Husbands. People like me."

He opened a huge Bible to a page marked with a velvet cord. "Mary washed his feet. Dried them with her long hair. How much more intimate can you be with our Lord? There were women in that last supper room, of course! Not just food servers! Disciples. Apostles. The writers of the Bible were like fish not seeing the water they swim in; they didn't see to include women's names."

Hillary's brain fired and she said, "But the names of Mary and Jesus' mother, when they found the tomb empty are mentioned."

"Indeed," Jean said. He nodded with closed eyes. "That is the true mystery. Why is it that in a few pivotal places, there are women. But someone had to be blamed for evil and death. Since she gives birth, which inevitably leads to death, the female is blamed."

Ed chewed his upper lip a few seconds, before he responded. "Crazy. Still, how does this help us find Claire?"

Jean frowned. "It seems clear that our god-fearing kidnappers chose women they see as taking away their power."

Ed nodded as Jean carried on, his voice harsh. "If I were to express these thoughts honestly, I would be excommunicated. But that's not all," Jean said. "At the conference, we mentioned incels as possible kidnappers. We skipped past them, but since Claire's gone missing, I've reconsidered."

He walked to the window and waved out at the Vatican spread out below. "Both the Roman church traditionalists," he said and turned to face Hillary. "And the involuntary celibates believe what they are entitled to is being stripped away, is under attack by newly liberated women. The incels seek to punish women for denying them sex. Who denies sex to men more than lesbians?"

Hillary crossed her arms over her chest and puffed out a long breath. "We argued. Claire stood up for incels. Said she forgives them. I can't picture them hurting her. But none of this helps find her. So, what if we understand or don't understand incels. She is still missing."

Ed said, "The missing women could be stand-ins

and blamed for the men's lack of success or just be targets for some other bizarre reasons."

It dawned on Hillary. "They want to force women back into subservient roles," she said, a feeling of horror spreading through her limbs. "Even rape them," she whispered.

Ed nodded. "I've been learning 8chan started out online as a sanctuary for male virgins who were enraged to think they would not ever get to have sex because women have become so choosy. It was supposed to be a positive space for men to see themselves as modern-day monks, but that led to violence and the UC Santa Barbara killings. I'm getting activity from IPs near some abandoned monasteries and trying to hack in closer. I am convinced that would be a perfect location for kidnappers to take their victims."

Jean said, "It's the church who denies sex to her priests. And the church has plenty of power, seen and unseen. I can't see incels at play here. I think it's a power play, could be Mafia." He picked up his phone. "I'm reaching out to my security clients." He began punching in buttons. "See what they're hearing."

Both men bristled with energy, going in different directions.

Hillary had to do something. Anything. "I'll call Jason Daniels and go to that wedding after all."

42
FATHER TOMMASO

Tommaso walked into the open lighted space to find Claire thrashing against the silk bindings that fastened her to the lounge, now turned back up and raised as a sort of gurney, waist high, as Tommaso had requested. She was flailing but silent. Tommaso knew the demon was waiting quietly inside, waiting to spring forth in its own time.

"I will need your assistance," he told the men. "Your witness." The four of them were the instruments of the Father.

Vito, Xavier, and Albert nodded, their faces grave. "Father, take care," Vito said, "that you don't become overwhelmed."

"Light the incense," Tommaso said to Xavier.

"Bring a pillow," he told Albert.

Tommaso held out his arms to let Vito pull the white surplice down over Tommaso's cassock.

Tommaso draped his green stole around his shoulders, and smoothed it, his big cross weighing the vestments down.

He faced Claire, whose hands twisted against her bindings. He made the sign of the cross over her, over himself, and over Vito, Xavier, and Albert.

He looked at Fredericka, sitting in the club chair with her head bowed, her lips moving silently. She was praying, he felt sure. Deep down, she was with them. He knew she would come around. Save herself and other women. He made the sign of the cross in her direction, as she mirrored the sacramental over herself.

Tommaso took the Cypress sprig he'd brought from the hillside and dipped it into the water he'd blessed in the other room. He sprinkled Claire, then all of them with holy water.

After this he prayed, "O Father God, I am sorry for having offended you, and I detest all my sins because of your just punishment, but most of all because they offend you, my God, who are all good and deserving of all my love. I resolve with the help of your grace to sin no more and to avoid the near occasion of sin. Amen.

He heaved a deep breath, held on to the edge of the long table, and knelt by Claire. He said, "Lord, have mercy." And waited to hear the response from the three men: "Christ, have mercy."

Claire groaned and jiggled her hips side to side.

Tommaso wiped the back of his hand across his forehead. "From all evil, deliver us, Lord." He waited for the three to echo his words.

"From all sin," they repeated.

"From the snares of the devil," they repeated after him.

"From all lewdness." Their echo pleased Tommaso.

"From the scourge of earthquakes." His heart was steady.

"From everlasting death." His heart was firm as he carried on the exorcism.

"We sinners, we beg you to hear us.

That you govern and preserve your holy Church,
and all ranks in the Church in holy religion.
That you humble the enemies of holy Church.
That you restore to the unity of the Church,
all who have embraced demons and strayed from the truth.
That you deliver our souls and the souls of our brethren
and benefactors from everlasting damnation."

Tommaso laid his right hand on Claire's chest and said, "Let the enemy have no power over her. And the son of iniquity be released from her."

Claire's chest hammered like a piston firing in an engine. Tommaso lifted up his hand a few inches. "Holy and everlasting God and Father, snatch from the clutches of the devil this, your servant, Claire, so the devil may no longer hold her captive."

Tommaso blinked fast. He thought he saw Claire's back arch, drawing her into the half circle of a rainbow, her feet sliding along the lounge toward her bound arms.

Vito looked unimpressed. Albert looked bored. Xavier looked like a man in love.

Tommaso shouted, "I command you, unclean spirit, whoever you are, along with all your minions now attacking this servant of God, by the mysteries of the incarnation, passion, resurrection, and ascension of our Lord Jesus Christ, by the descent of the Holy Spirit, by the coming of our Lord for judgment, that you tell me by some sign your name, and the day and hour of your departure."

Tommaso waited. He listened. A faint crooning was what he heard.

"I command you to obey me to the letter, I, who am a minister of God despite my unworthiness; nor shall you be emboldened to harm in any way this creature of God, or the bystanders, or any of their possessions."

Tommaso placed his hand on Claire's head. He said, "They shall lay their hands upon the sick and all will be well with them. At that time, the seventy-two returned in high spirits. 'Master,' they said, 'even the demons are subject to us because we use your name!'"

Cries poured from Claire's throat, and she tossed her head side to side. Tommaso raised his hand and spread out his fingers into a five-pointed star. "Jesus said to them, 'I was watching Satan fall like lightning that flashes from heaven'."

Tommaso raised his open hand high and whisked it down and back up. Claire's face was turning red. Tommaso made the sign of the cross over himself and over her. He placed the end of his green stole on her neck, and his right hand on her head.

He felt something pull at his chest as he cried, "I cast you out, unclean spirit, along with every Satanic power of the enemy, every specter from hell, and all your companions, in the name of our Lord. Begone and stay far from this creature of God. For it is He who commands you, He who flung you headlong from the heights of heaven into the depths of hell. It is He who commands you, He who stilled the sea and the wind and the storm."

The lights flickered in the open lighted place. "... tremble in fear, Satan. Repel, 0 Lord, the devil's power, break asunder his snares and traps, put the unholy tempter to flight. By the sign," he said and traced a cross on Claire's brow. "Of your name, let this, your servant Claire, be protected in mind and body."

Claire had bitten through her gag and was

shouting at him. "You're crazy, crazy!" Tommaso thought he saw spittle shooting from her lips. He pulled the cross off from his neck and stuck it between her teeth, silencing her.

He traced a cross on her chest and said, "Let vanish from her soul the voice of the evil spirit, may himself retreat in terror and defeat, and no more terrorize us. Keep watch over the inmost recesses of her heart, rule over her emotions, strengthen her will."

Tommaso's throat stung. He clutched his neck. "Yield, yield not to my own person …" He bent over in a coughing fit, tears running down his cheeks, his head throbbing.

The floor shook. "Tremble before the mighty arm that broke apart dark prison walls and led souls forth to light. May the trembling that afflicts this human frame…" He struggled to stand upright and reached to make the sign of the cross on Claire's chest.

"Do not think …" He worked to take a breath. "Of despising my command…" His chest wouldn't move. "… You know me to be a great sinner."

He was paralyzed, but his lips were moving. "The continence of the confessors commands you. The prayers of holy men command you."

Claire seemed to be growling. Tommaso thought he could see foam at the corners of her mouth, his cross digging into her cheek.

Gasping for air, Tommaso kept going. "Depart, creature, give way, monster, give way to Christ, who has stripped you of your powers and laid waste your kingdom. He has cast you forth into outer darkness, where everlasting ruin awaits you and those…."

Vito cried out, "Father, take care!"

Tommaso could hear growling from deep inside himself.

43
FATHER TOMMASO

The lights flickered and went out. Tommaso was wheezing, trying to draw in a breath. "You are guilty before the whole human race, whom you tempted by your cup of death. I command you depart from this woman." He felt for her brow. Claire's head was jerking back and forth. With his thumb, Tommaso made a cross on her forehead.

Fredericka pulled at his stole. "Father, stop! You are acting out the evil when women knew their place, obeyed every directive, and never questioned the Church had all the answers about life, here and hereafter!"

Vito called out, "Father, this is killing you!"

Tommaso turned to where the three men stood. "Depart from the Church of God." He made the sign of the cross in their direction. "And from me, your faithful servant." Tommaso crossed himself with a shaking hand.

"Tremble and flee, as we call on the name of the Lord, before him the denizens of hell cower. Jesus of Nazareth commands you to enter into a herd of pigs."

Tommaso clutched his belly and doubled over. A hoarse voice bellowed out through his throat, "Who's out bleeding in the vineyard?"

He heard a thump.

"Claire's escaped," screamed Xavier.

Vito slipped his arm under Tommaso's chest. "Claire jumped off the lounge and sprinted down the tunnel."

Tommaso worked to get his breath. "Bring … her … back," he whispered.

Vito followed the young men down the tunnel.

Tommaso staggered to the deck chair and closed his eyes, willing himself to ignore the clutch of pain in his gut. He listened for them to capture and carry the shrieking Claire back in and gag and bind her back up on the gurney.

He stood. There was Vito holding her feet, and Albert with his arms pinning her down. Xavier stood at the side, tears running down his cheeks.

Tommaso put his hand on Claire's brow. "The evil one is driving you into the everlasting fire. For you, his follower, mother of lechery, model of vileness, inventor of every obscenity, there will be worms that never die. We diligently worked to expel the darkness from you, to get your confession, but you have denied everything.

"We have tried to induce you to repent; but you being obstinately given over to wickedness have scorned our advice and have persisted with stubborn and defiant mind.

"The Church of God has implored the devil to leave you and for you to repent and acknowledge your guilt, and you have refused. God's grace and mercy can go no farther."

Claire's bound shoulders thrashed, and howls poured from her throat.

Tommaso stood trembling as he felt warm urine run down his leg.

"So that you may be an example to others that they may be kept from such heresies, and that such crimes may not remain unpunished and having before our eyes only our Father God, we pronounce you an impenitent heretic and consigned to the fire!"

Bursting forth in a hoarse whisper, Xavier said, "If she is bound to the place she is to be burned, and then she should confess the truth and acknowledge her guilt, she still may in mercy be received as a penitent and her life and soul be saved. Right, Father?"

Tommaso staggered into the other room, the tearful Xavier at his side. Xavier said, "The fire is the only way to save her soul?"

Tommaso leaned against the altar and whispered, "She's a witch. Got to burn the devil out of her."

Xavier's face turned pale.

"Go, my son, make a clearing in the vineyard, pile up dead leaves. We must purify her soul."

44
HILLARY

Hillary's eyes popped open. She lay unmoving in bed. Her heart raced. She squeezed her hands into fists, her nails dug into her palms. *We will find you, Claire. Hold on.*

She forced herself to get up. It was hot. She fluttered the straps of her nightgown, fanning a breeze on her sweaty skin. Ed sat on the loveseat, pounding away at his keyboard. His fingers flew. He stabbed the return key and said, "I just backdoored my way into a dark forum. Now to poke around for hints of kidnappings." He looked up at her. "Is Jason going with you to that wedding? I don't want you going alone."

She gave a moan.

Ed stood and wrapped his arms around her. She collapsed against his chest. "Argggggg, our girl. Where is she?"

He pulled her down to the loveseat. "We will find her," he said massaging her shoulders. He held her as she sobbed. "We made her, and we will find her. She's our flesh and blood."

After long minutes, he wiped her cheeks with his white tee shirt. She laughed hysterically. "Where are your white handkerchiefs when I really need them?"

She gazed at his face, his green eyes. Safety. There was safety here. She licked her finger and traced the dark auburn of his eyebrows, tapping on that one white hair.

"We will find her," Ed said. "I feel good about my new leads in the incel forums, even if Jean discredits them. Is Jason going with you to that wedding?'

The corners of her lips turned down. She nodded. "He wants to try and make up for ..." Her breath caught in her throat. "For losing track of Claire. We can look for faces and hiding places."

"Can't hurt to check it out," Ed said.

Hillary steeled herself for the day ahead, another day without her daughter. She phoned Sofia and asked if they had anything new.

Sofia said, "Powerful men don't get their hands dirty—there is never a direct connection to their crimes. But we are tracking them. It won't hurt to check out that wedding. The *Daily Bread* podcast has urged listeners to go protest. They are running quotes from Genesis 2:24 and Matthew 19:5 that marriage is a union between one man and one woman."

Hillary disconnected. She fiddled with her Mary medal. She would go to that wedding, do her own kind of tracking.

. . .

A WEDDING STAFFER DIPPED HIS HEAD IN GREETING and waved them in. Hillary searched the faces of guests, making it seem as if she was simply admiring the pond, the greenery below the high stone walls, the worn sculptures of classical figures. It looked like a place out of a fairy tale. Or a horror story.

Could Claire be a captive here? She walked over to the staffer. "What an interesting place. Does this monastery have catacombs?"

"No. It has tombs, but most were robbed long ago. The below-ground ones have been covered over, so no one falls in. Safety is a big concern."

She nodded.

"You might wonder why the roof is gone from between the arches?" He pointed up to the gothic arches. They made Hillary think of the ribs of a huge bird. "Earthquakes," he said. "Most of the ceiling collapsed over time. The rubble's been carried off long ago."

Hillary nodded. Earthquakes. Rubble. What if Claire was trapped inside a place like this? She followed Jason into the sanctuary. With the roof gone, sunlight painted golden bands across faded frescos on stone walls. Rows of folding chairs had been set up.

Jason led the way to the far side, near wooden confessional booths that looked to Hillary like coffins standing on end. She sat and turned to study the faces of guests coming in through the gap that once held massive double doors.

When the sanctuary was nearly full, violins began pouring out a lively melody. Hillary looked at Jason with raised eyebrows. He whispered it was from *La Traviata*, about a fallen woman.

Down the aisle came two little girls, solemn faced, their blond hair swept back and pinned with white carnations. They held a pink basket between them and with their free hands pulled out red petals, throwing them ahead. Hillary flashed back to the summer Claire was seven, how adorable she was, exploring old castles in Ireland. *Where is she now?*

Without warning, a fist-sized piece from an overhead arch broke loose and landed in front of the girls. They squealed and stopped to look down at the face of a plaster angel beaming up at them.

What might be falling on Claire at this moment? Hillary's heart raced as the violins played on.

A staffer hurried to scoop up the fallen piece. He pivoted to carry it down the aisle and out a side door. The little girls giggled and resumed their steps toward the ancient altar, threaded with ivy.

The violin music swelled, and the guests' eyes turned to the back. And there she was. The bride. Her black hair fell over her white bodice, tight against her breasts—a young woman in a cloud of white netting, clutching a bouquet of red roses, a regal figure, as if commanding the sun to bless this, her wedding day. She turned to an older woman beside her. Her mother. Hillary's eyes filled with tears. Her mother walked her down the aisle.

A tall redhead in a sheath of shimmering black satin waited at the vine-covered altar. The bride kissed her mother and stepped up to stand next to her betrothed. A woman in a clerical collar led the couple through a ceremony that struck Hillary as surprisingly traditional.

When the officiant asked who knows why this couple should not be joined together, the silence seemed long with possibility. Were any of those *Daily Bread* followers here to speak up?

The clergywoman took the hands of the couple, joined them and placed her own on top. "By the divine love that brings you here and by the vows you have pledged, it is my honor to pronounce you partners for life."

For life. Where was Claire? Was she alive? What was Hillary doing here? She should be combing the streets. Where could she look for her daughter?

The newlyweds pranced down the aisle, hands clasped and raised high as the violins played the Wedding March.

Outside, Hillary said, "I don't think I can stand this. It's crazy to think anyone connected to the kidnappers or protestors would come to this."

Jason adjusted his crossover bag and waved at the tables set up. "We're here now. Let's stay and look over the crowd."

She sat and studied the fifty or so people waiting

for the brides to join the reception, checking for signs like those at the funeral. But this place hadn't seemed to attract hate showing its face.

The brides waltzed in to the cheers of the crowd. They stood at a head table and raised champagne flutes. A man and a woman in operatic costumes ran in and bowed in front of them. Off to the side, the violinists materialized and played as the costumed couple sang with gusto in Italian. Some guests mouthed the lyrics as the music soared.

Jason whispered, "It's the Brindizi. A drinking song, for a toast."

The brides tapped their flutes in a salute then raised them to toast their guests. "Cin cin! Salute! Let's drink from joyful cups! May all our moments be voluptuous!" They sipped their champagne. "Let's delight in love."

Hillary couldn't summon any joyful energy to lift her glass off the table, set with bottles of wine, one a straw-wrapped bottle of Chianti. Jason picked it up and said, "Did you know we call this a *fiasco*?"

She heaved a sigh. That's what this trip to Italy had turned into. A fiasco. "Let's get out of here," she said.

As Jason led their way out, she saw ahead of them an old man, stooped and holding a white satin bag that some guests were putting envelopes into. "Who's that?" she asked Jason.

"He must be one of the brides' grandfathers. The custom is to put envelopes with money into the bag.

It's called 'la borsa.' The grandfathers have the honor of holding it. I brought something for it."

Jason pulled an envelope from his crossover bag. As she looked down toward the satin bag, Hillary spotted a red and white card with no envelope. She gasped and looked up at him. "It's, it's …" She couldn't stop herself and lifted the card out. An oval of red hearts bordered five lines:

The Catechism
of the Catholic Church
states that homosexual acts
are intrinsically
disordered

Jason put his envelope into the satin bag and took the card from Hillary's fingers. "Those people. They think they mean well. But, no need for that quote today." He tore the card in two, put it into his crossover bag and moved toward the parking lot.

Her jaw clenched, Hillary nodded. There were haters here after all. Cowards this time. They must have already left.

On the way to Jason's car, she passed by a sun-bleached sculpture of the goddess Clementia. There she was again. Clemency, mercy and forgiveness. No way.

. . .

Back at the convent, Hillary went to the chapel and the same place she sat before. It must be Pauline in the pew across the narrow aisle, gazing down at the stone floor, her face obscured by her blue veil.

Hillary picked up the prayer book and thumbed through it. She didn't know what page to turn to. Pauline didn't look her way. She could be praying for SisterFredericka. Maybe the missing nun usually sat where Hillary was now. Closing her eyes, Hillary tried to relax into the silence. Soon, the rise and fall of women praying surrounded her in a soothing embrace. She breathed in *Find* and breathed out *Claire*. Find. Claire. Find. Claire.

After evening prayers, Hillary asked Pauline if she had a few minutes to talk. The nun nodded and said, "Let's go to the roof. It's cool now. The cicadas are done for the day." They took the creaky elevator to the 4th floor rooftop garden and sat in the canvas covered swing. Pauline nodded at Hillary, inviting her to speak.

"I know we are supposed to love one another, but I hate whoever kidnapped Claire. I hate myself for letting her go. When we prayed at Trota's funeral, I vowed not to forgive those kidnappers." She stared at Pauline with her eyes unblinking, brows raised high.

Pauline nodded.

"I saw Clementia again today," Hillary said. "A sculpture at the wedding. I can't feel clemency, forgiveness, but I feel guilty about that. You know, in the Lord's Prayer when we pray to forgive those who trespass against us?"

Pauline nodded again.

"When I first learned that prayer, we said 'debts and debtors' instead of 'trespasses and trespass against us.' Debtors." Hillary sighed.

Pauline let the silence stretch out.

"For years," Hillary said, "I haven't been able to forgive the debt my mother owes me. She left me abandoned." Tears rolled down Hillary's cheeks. "She never said she was sorry. Then I could..." She heaved in a long sob and shuddered. "Maybe forgive her."

Pauline put her hand on Hillary's shoulder and said, "You are not alone. It takes a lifetime to learn to forgive. You think your mother has to change, apologize before you can forgive her, but maybe she's not the one who needs to change." Pauline rocked the swing gently with her foot as minutes passed.

"I've been a bad mother, too," Hillary whispered and stared wild-eyed at Pauline. "Not holding on to my child."

"Does your mother realize that Claire has been kidnapped?"

Hillary's jaw sagged. "I don't know," she said.

Pauline raised her eyebrows. "Maybe let her know? Ask for help, even?"

Hillary folded her lips in on themselves and rocked back and forth in the swing. Maybe her mother felt like this some of the time. Never let on about it. Being a bad mother. She sniffed, pulled a white hanky from her pocket and blew her nose. I should forgive her. And I will.

Pauline got up and left.

Hillary took out her phone. She texted Paisley.

Did you hear what happened? Claire's been kidnapped. We could use your help.

She stared at the screen, her heart beating slow and loud in time with the crickets. She read the message aloud to herself. What kind of help might her mother be? Should she reach out like this? Maybe Paisley wouldn't care to come help. Hillary paced the flat floor of the rooftop and stared at the waxing crescent moon. Luna. Lunatic. This was crazy.

She read the message out loud again. There's nothing really to lose, is there?

She hit Send.

Hillary couldn't eat more than a couple bites of the Mortadella Panini Ed had picked up. She had a couple glasses of Sangiovese and watched Ed surf the dark web. She was shocked at the vitriol and violence expressed in so many ways on the forums.

Lots of fantasizing about rape and torture but nothing about kidnapping and hiding women away.

After a couple hours of searching, Ed took a break. She told him about her text to Paisley. "I've got my fingers crossed, Genevieve," he said and went back to searching for any mention of abductions or snatches or nabs or other possible terms for kidnapping.

Hillary changed into her thin summer nighty and kept her eye on her phone, ready to pick up a reply from Paisley.

By midnight, crickets had notched up their volume, but she'd had no chirps from her phone. She stretched and yawned. "I'm giving up on a relationship with my mother," she said, "Forget an apology, forgiving her or ever getting close."

"I'm with you, Genevieve, I'm here," Ed said, enfolding her in his arms while she sobbed.

---

45
HILLARY

In the darkness, Hillary woke. "Mamma. Mamma!" She clapped her hand over her mouth. Ed was snoring his gentle rhythms. The room was black. *Mamma*. Where did that come from?

Sweating, she pushed off the duvet and rubbed her hand over the damp front of her nightgown. She stepped barefoot onto the cool tile floor. Her phone lay silent on the bedside table. She reached to tap it and check the time—3:05 a.m.

And there it was: A text message from Paisley.

> The gallery owner Paul heard that our Claire was taken. I'm coming down on the train.

Hillary rubbed her eyes. She read the message again and ran her thumbs over the cold face of the phone.

The message had just been sent one minute ago.

Hot anger flooded Hillary's chest. A gallery owner convinced Paisley to come help. Not the plea from Hillary. She went into the cramped bathroom, closed the door and turned on the light over the sink.

Hillary

Do you know where we are staying?

Paisley

In Rome somewhere.

Hillary closed the toilet seat lid and sat. To stop her hands from shaking, she pressed her thumbs hard against the phone before she texted back.

Hillary

I'll meet your train. What time does it get to Termini?

Paisley

I'm going to Tiburina. Less expensive.

Hillary shook her head. What a time to worry about money.

Hillary

I'll pay you back for the ticket.

Paisley

Of course not! Pick me up at Tiburina.
Paul gave me an idea to find Claire.

Hillary leaned back and rubbed her closed eyes. Paul. An art gallery owner. What could he know?

A new line showed up on the phone screen.

Paisley

Are you still there?

Am I still here? After all these years? I have no choice. We need all the help we can get to find Claire.

Hillary was shocked to see Paisley look so joyful when she picked her up from the Tiburnia. "So, what does this Paul think will help find Claire?" Hillary asked once they were back on the road.

"It's genius, my dear. Along with his focus on the theft of art objects, Paul follows true crime stories. Last year, fifteen thousand foreigners went missing in Italy. He's upset it gets little attention."

"Wow."

"Yes, well, Paul works with the Carabinieri on art theft cases. Apparently, there is a new crime called 'artnapping,' would you believe. Stealing art and holding it for ransom until the gallery, museum, or private owner pays to retrieve it. If the ransom is not paid, thieves destroy the artwork to avoid the risk of being caught. Since stolen art is recovered by way of images, Paul suggests we get an image of Claire up onto the art theft pipeline. He thinks that could send out a tendril, possibly turn up something."

"Hmmm. She *was* with an artist when she was kidnapped."

"Paul said you should ask the police if they've tried that tactic."

"I'll run it by Sofia and Mario."

"Good. Now that I'm here, what can I do?"

What can she do? There was so much Paisley had never done. Hillary was at a loss for words. "Let's get an update from Ed."

Back at the suite, Ed was on the phone when they arrived. Hillary couldn't help but stare at Claire's alcove and her bright shorts, skirts and tops of many colors, all hanging loose now. Claire's absence was screaming into the room.

Paisley cleared her throat. Hillary turned and gestured at the two chairs across from Ed. He set his phone down and stood, holding out his arms. "Welcome back, Paisley!"

They hugged, and he said, "You're here to help find our girl, yes?"

"What can I do?"

Ed turned to Hillary. "That was Jean on the

phone. I'm going with him to Valdos Verde, talk to one of his Security clients."

"A client? Who?"

"A cafe owner. She wants to see us. Jean thinks she suspects Claire's kidnapping could be Mafia related, even though we've not had any ransom demands." Ed's eyes were narrowed.

"Why doesn't she just call the police?"

"His client is afraid of the Polizia and doesn't trust telling them anything."

"Can we come?"

"You stay on watch here, check in with Sofia, see if there's any progress." He gave her a bear hug, threw on a lightweight jacket, and left.

The silence in the room grew heavy. It was time. "Why come to be with me now?" Hillary asked.

"Because I love Claire," Paisley said and walked over to her suitcase. She opened a side pocket and pulled out an envelope. "And because …" She pulled a letter from the envelope, unfolded it, and handed it to Hillary. "I've been nominated. It's for the Guggenheim Prize for influential art."

Hillary glanced at the letter. At the bottom of the page was a scene of a sunset over a fiery ocean. She threw a puzzled look at Paisley.

"I don't have to yearn for respect anymore," Paisley said, "like when you were young, and I was stuck at home with your Pulitzer Prize-winning father."

Hillary was stunned. "You weren't winning prizes,

so you deserted me?" She stood. "Left me abandoned ..." She threw open her arms. "Like an open wound, bandaging myself behind a curtain of lies?" She crossed her arms over her chest and glared at Paisley. "One thing you need to know is that I told everyone you were dead. I made up a story about how you were out painting in your studio, and I went to tell you I was hungry. You lashed out at me with your paint-brush, poking me in the cheeks and telling me I was getting fat, too fat, that I needed to stop thinking about food all the time. I said you got so worked up about it that your face turned red and you started gasping and clutching at your throat."

Paisley kept hold of the letter and watched as Hillary paced the floor, talking fast.

"I said you fell to the floor holding your brush and your palate in your hands and the palate of paint landed on the front of your dress and the red paint made it look like you were stabbed in the heart." Hillary pounded her chest.

"I said I ran out of the studio and back to the house. I phoned Daddy at work, and he told me to call 911. The ambulance came, and I said they worked on you for an hour, but you were dead. I said I threw myself on your body and cried and cried until Daddy came home and picked me up and told me you had to be taken away in a van to the funeral home." Hillary stopped talking. She stood directly in front of Paisley. Hillary bent forward until her face was six inches from the face of her mother.

She said very slowly, "Couldn't you at least tell me you are sorry?"

Paisley waved the letter out to the side. "Do you recognize the painting at the bottom of the letter?" Paisley sang out.

"Why would I?" Hillary did recall seeing a scene like that in the cottage studio last month when she'd gone to ask Paisley to help keep Claire safe.

"I sent you cards I painted for you, inviting you to fly over and live with me in Tahiti's tropical paradise."

"I never got anything like that."

"Jake threw them out."

A pang hit Hillary. She walked away, masking her hurt for a moment, but turning to face Paisley, she said, "You painted cards for me, but Daddy … you're saying he threw them away? How would you know that?"

Paisley unzipped another pocket of her suitcase. "I kept this." She slid a card out and held it next to the letter. The images were the same. She opened the card.

Hillary stared at what she saw, a handwritten note inviting her to go live with her mother. Paisley turned the card to the back side.

There, in Jake's block printing was his message.

JOANNA. STOP SENDING THESE PIECES OF JUNK. NO MAIL COMES TO OUR HOUSE. I'VE GOT A PO BOX. HILLARY WILL NEVER READ ANY OF YOUR PATHETIC MESSAGES. YOU WILL NEVER SUCCEED AT ANYTHING. JAKE.

"Jake sent this card back to me by return mail. He must have destroyed all the others I sent over the years."

Hillary's jaw hung open.

"I even took it to court, but I lost the case. From then on, I worked to perfect my paintings of the sunset, out of sorrow that our time was over. Sorrow." There were tears in her eyes.

Hillary frowned and took a few deep breaths. "All this time I've spent holding a grudge against you."

Paisley pursed her lips and then spoke. "When you called me a narcissist, I took it as an element to add to the sunset, focus on a single image. I began to wonder if it was a sunset or a sunrise. That painting of that ordinary subject has put me in the running to win the Guggenheim Hugo prize." She added softly, "The title is, 'Forgive me, but it was not my fault.' Words cannot express how sorry I am, so I use paint instead, my daughter."

Hillary was flushed with grief and relief, mixed together, as if a peppermint hot pepper shower had fallen over her. "I'm the one who's sorry for blaming you alone. I can't blame him because he's dead. I see it differently now."

She opened her arms to her mother. Paisley reached out and they stood in a long hug, wordless, in the hot Italian afternoon.

Later, Hillary waved in the direction of the hallway. "Let's go see if anyone has heard anything about finding our Claire."

Standing a few inches from Paisley as the old elevator creaked its way down, Hillary took shallow breaths, not used to being so close to her mother. She searched for a topic of conversation. "The nuns here are pretty amazing," she said. "Maybe Sister Pauline will be taking her turn in the lobby. She's a kind of artist. She told me she's going to create an Illuminated Bible."

"Oh, is she using gold leaf?"

"Not sure, but …" The white enamel door jerked its way open. Hillary stepped out, free from the tiny cage.

Running down the hallway toward her was Sister Pauline, her blue veil flying behind her.

"Ms. Broome! I have a message! Mother Catherine says you should go talk to Aunt Eleanora in Sotto Voce village."

Pauline stopped to catch her breath. "She says Eleanora saw the photo of Claire on TV. Later that night, she saw somebody looks like her in her tenant's car in her courtyard. Eleanora doesn't trust the police. Mother C. says you should hurry! Her aunt manages an apartment. It's called Piedi Collina, at the foot of a hill."

46
XAVIER

Xavier sent Albert to collect a hand saw and wire cutters from the shed. From the church steps, Xavier looked out over the skeletal vines, wrapped around wires their lives had depended on. The wires and brittle vines still clung to pine scaffolding, built to the height of a man for tending and harvesting the Sangiovese grapes, the vines trained onto the wires with twine and bungees.

The good old days when Father Joseph supervised the crush and the long process for turning the grapes into communion wine. He fingered the olive wood crucifix around his neck and sighed.

Albert returned with an old saw and some wire cutters. He stood looking over the dead vines. "It looks like a whole field of crucifixions, those dead branches clinging to wooden crosses."

Xavier sent Albert to haul one of the old rubber hoses from the shed over to the front of the church.

Xavier threaded the hose onto the spigot. It was long past time to save the grapes, but they didn't want to set the whole vineyard on fire. Plus, they needed to put out the fire as soon as Claire confessed.

This would be a first, and he wasn't sure how to go about it. He knew how to manage the fires inside the monastery, the wood-fired downdraft kiln for the clay burial plaques and the wood-fired oven for baking bread.

He'd researched online, but this was not the same as the Inquisition fires for punishment in Spain. Not at all. Father Tommaso intended this to get Claire to confess, to save her, not to punish her. To put the fear of God into her. Not to kill her.

Xavier didn't plan to match what he saw on the fresco in the church and on the covers of Father Joseph's *Malleus* books. He visualized instead a simple pyramid of sticks on the ground.

He went out to the row of grapes nearest the church and cut the rusty wires and brittle vines away from the pine crossarms attached to the first upright post.

He set a few dry vines and leaves in a four-foot square of sun-dried dirt at the foot of the post. The vines and leaves, plus a few grapes hardened to raisins would be good kindling. He had Albert help him arrange three crossarm pieces against the base of the 4x4, positioning them in a sort of pyramid. He wanted just sparse kindling. Didn't want the thing to get out of control, really burn her. Just get her to confess.

He stepped back and studied his work. He prayed Claire would not be stubborn.

Albert dragged over another armload of crossarm pieces. “Got to put in more wood.”

“No,” Xavier said. “She’ll confess and repent when the first flames tickle her toes.”

“I’ll throw more on if she balks,” Albert said, throwing his armload of wooden slats down near the post.

Xavier gritted his teeth. They had to get her to confess quickly, save her soul. And her body. Become a real woman, marry a man and raise a family.

47
HILLARY

Hillary ran to the car park, Paisley a few steps behind. Hillary punched Voce Sotto into the GPS. She pulled out of the lot, tires screeching. "Text Ed," she said and tossed her phone to her mother.

"What do I tell him?"

"We are driving to Voce Sotto to see Aunt Eleanora."

Paisley poked the message onto the screen with her index finger.

On the motorway, Hillary floored the accelerator. "Go ahead and text Sofia, since Ed's not replying. Her number's in my phone." Hillary's thoughts jumped from one idea to another.

"See if you can find BBC news on the radio. I should have gotten that reporter's phone number."

"Why are we going to Voce Sotto? What's there?" Paisley asked.

"I don't know. I'm just trusting Sister Pauline. I've never met Mother Catherine. I've seen her from a distance, looks around 50 maybe, so her aunt must be up there in years. Mother Catherine stays in the back of the convent, secluded."

Paisley snorted a laugh. "Secluded! I was secluded when I was nineteen! No more days out demonstrating on the Capitol steps. Jake kept me barefoot and pregnant. Life was different in the 70s." She sighed.

"You're plenty free now, and winning awards, too. Let's stick to finding Claire. So, Mother Catherine's aunt's name is Eleanora. She's the manager of an apartment building in a little village. Pauline said that Mother Catherine hardly ever comments on anything in the news. It's weird she would ask Pauline to tell me to go talk to this aunt."

"Families," Paisley said. "Aunties and nieces, mothers and daughters. Could be some paintings there."

Paintings. Hillary's heart fluttered. She glanced at her mother. "Have you ever seen a painting of the Madonna holding a girl baby?"

"Not exactly, but one of the other finalists for the Guggenheim has a huge oil of the Madonna holding a dying female across her lap."

Hillary gulped. "What do you make of that?"

"Bob Dylan was right. The times are a-changing, and faster than ever."

Hillary stared at the straight stretch of motorway,

willing the car to go faster. She barely glanced at the vineyards and olive groves dotting the Tuscan countryside she sped through.

"Anything from Ed? Do we have service?" she asked Paisley.

"Nothing. No service."

Hillary turned up the radio.

> *This is an alert, alert. American teen vanished from Roman pizza parlor, 15 years old, short blond hair, petite athletic build, wearing a Love Wins rainbow pride tee shirt. Call 118 if you have seen or heard anything that might be connected. In other news...*

Hillary put the gas pedal to the floor. Speeding tickets be damned. What might Zia Eleanora have to tell them?

48
XAVIER

Xavier knew better than to disturb Father Tommaso. He was in the altar room, praying. He'd said he would come out when the time was right.

Xavier checked on Fredericka, loosely tied into her lounge and looking serene. Why did the nun seem so unperturbed? He turned toward Claire's niche.

Fredericka called out to Xavier, "Don't deny that flash of interest in your eyes, young man. Faces don't lie. I've always been right about that."

Xavier felt blood rush to his cheeks, grateful his beard had grown to spare him embarrassment, blushing like the virgin he was. He cleared his throat. "Albert and I have the wood ready outside, but I'm hoping she confesses before he lights the fire."

"He is not really going through with that?" Fredericka tugged at her silk scarf ties. "How archaic! Burning at the stake. Ridiculous."

Xavier pursed his lips and pulled at the short hairs of his beard. “Not to kill her. Persuade her to confess. Save her soul with the threat of hellfire.”

“That’s not going to persuade someone like Claire.”

Albert looked up from where he sat at the table surfing forums on his laptop. He said, “Bitches and witches are persuaded with pain. Getting tattooed or the threat of rape. I’m good at both. She’d confess then. No need for the mess of a fire.”

Fredericka asked, “Why would tattooing make people confess?”

Albert grinned, and said, “When I lived in New York, I hung out at a tattoo studio. I did the dirty work, mopped the floor, made the inks, answered phones, so the owner let me watch him work. I learned how to benefit from putting people through pain. Getting them to agree to things is not hard. You listen to them talk about their painful life experiences. In this vulnerable situation, they beg for things they need and want at a deep level.”

He laughed. “I’m good at the other thing, too. Get her pregnant, she’d change. Be what a woman should be.” Albert walked back to the altar room doorway. “What do you say, Father Tommaso? Want me to try my way to convince Claire? A tat or a rape would let you skip the fiery mess in the vineyard.”

Tommaso heaved out a long, loud breath, and then in a hoarse voice, he yelled, “No, never!” He coughed. “The devil’s getting into you, son.”

Albert stomped off. Surprised and shaking his head in disapproval at Albert's suggestion, Xavier muttered, "Fazzo."

49
HILLARY

There it was, painted on the door—Piedi Collina. *Ufficio Affitto Appartamenti.* Apartment Rental Office. Hillary clutched her tote against her side, opened the door and walked in past a wooden bench against the wall. A woman in a black shawl sat bent over a small table, stringing beads onto a silver wire.

"Buona sera," Hillary said. Paisley echoed the greeting.

"Salve." The woman said and walked to a stand holding jewelry. She pointed to the bracelets and necklaces, a smile on her wrinkled face.

Hillary shook her head. "Scusa, not shopping today."

The old woman wagged her hands, palms down. "No appartamento libero."

Hillary's blood ran cold. Surely the woman spoke English? "Mother Catherine sent me to find Zia

Eleanora. She saw someone in a car in the courtyard? My daughter Claire is missing. I am Hillary."

"Ah. Illarie." She turned and disappeared into a back room.

The woman had made her name sound like "ill are we." Hillary's stomach cramped. She jumped when Paisley rubbed her shoulder and said, "The woman is an artist." She nodded at the jewelry on the stand. "Exquisite work."

Hillary blew out her lips. "This is no time for shopping."

Paisley smiled. "Here she comes."

The old woman carried a flat beaded purse, beaming as if presenting a birthday cake with candles aflame. "Questo è per te." She transferred the purse to one hand and bent to hold it close to Hillary.

Hillary looked at Paisley, who said, "Take it." Hillary reached out her palms and received the purse. She sat on the bench, her heart pounding, looking from the purse to the old woman.

"Apri, apri," Zia Eleanora said, one hand twisting over the top of the purse, motioning for Hillary to open it.

Hillary opened the purse and pulled out some papers. They looked like official documents, in Italian. She looked at Zia Eleanora with raised eyebrows. "Non parlo italiano. Did you see a girl in the courtyard?"

Zia Eleanora crossed her arms over her chest. A scowl contorted her features. She opened the door and limped out to the courtyard. She pointed to a black Lancia and waved a follow-me gesture at Hillary, before she darted to her left and disappeared around a corner.

Hillary slipped the documents back into the flat purse and put it in her tote. She checked to make sure her water bottle was fastened tight. Couldn't get the purse wet.

"Let's go, Mamma," she said to Paisley. She looked in the windows of the black Lancia to make sure no one was in it before she ran in the direction Zia Eleanora had gone.

Hillary could barely see the old woman, waving at her from far away. She was in a dirt clearing half a football field distant, at the base of a tall hillside. She pointed at a pathway and began yelling. Hillary ran closer and could make her words out. "Monastero! Vai lassù, vai lassù!"

Hillary's heart was racing. "We are supposed to go up there?" She waved her arm at the wooded incline.

Zia Eleanora's head was bobbing up and down. "Si, si." She stamped her feet. "Monastero!"

"Holy Mary! Where's your phone?"

"In my bra," Paisley said, clapping her chest.

"Do you have phone service yet, Mamma?"

Paisley checked her phone. "No."

"We'll just have to hope Ed got that earlier text," Hillary said. "If this is the place, and Claire is here, so are the kidnappers. What kind of weapons do we have? I was stupid not to think about that before!"

Hillary pawed through her tote. "And you don't even carry a bag.

"Here's the car key." Hillary slipped the metal key out from the remote-control fob it was fastened inside.

"And a pen and my phone. Not much." Her shoulders sagged. "Phones aren't weapons."

"But," Paisley tugged at the cord of her necklace. "Light and lethal."

Hillary stared. "What?"

"My *ka'ane.*" She nodded. "I told you, I keep it handy. Slip it off, stretch it out and voila, it's a strangling cord."

Hillary's eyes opened wide. "Wow," she breathed.

"Pull it tight, it's a garrote." Paisley stretched out the ends of the cord. "Let it go, the bad man can speak again."

Hillary nodded. She clicked her ball point pen shut and slid it into her bra. She positioned the car key, jagged end facing down, between her middle and ring finger. "Let's go see what's up there." She took a deep breath. "Or who."

50
FATHER TOMMASO

Tommaso took the lighter out from his cassock pocket. He flicked it and bent to hold the flame to a dead leaf clinging to a wisp of a faded vine.

He waited for the leaf to catch fire before he called out, "Confess your sins, your lustful cravings."

Claire's guttural calls responded.

He wiped his sweaty face with the back of his hand. "Take off the gag," he told Xavier, who did as he was told.

"You can't do this!" She screamed. "This is crazy! You're insane!"

"Truth is always truth. You are bewitched. We beg you confess before you become insensible to the pain of the flames."

"Love is not a sin! We are to love one another!"

"Do not die before you confess! You have a choice!"

"I confess to loving women and helping others to be proud, but not by witchcraft. This is not a sin!"

"Confess and repent!" Tommaso fanned the base of the fire with the skirt of his cassock, the low flames dancing nearer Claire's feet.

51
HILLARY

Hillary hurried up the path through the densely wooded hillside of spruce, chestnut, and oak groves. She stumbled near a giant oak and fell flat on her face. Lifting her head, she clawed oak leaves away to find a gap in the soil the size of a Dutch oven.

"Watch out," she called to Paisley, close behind her. "The ground's uneven—probably wild pigs rooting for truffles."

She dusted herself off and turned away from the view of the Tuscan countryside. She doubled her pace hiking up the path.

The climb was steeper than it looked. She ignored the temptation to stop a moment at one of the dilapidated wooden benches. Paisley didn't stop to rest either.

After twenty minutes walking fast as she could, Hillary was breathing hard. She slowed as the slope flattened out. Trees gave way to rows of withered vines stretched out across a dry field.

"A vineyard." She turned to Paisley. "Do you smell smoke?"

Paisley wrinkled her nose and sniffed. "Yes."

"A vineyard…on fire?"

Paisley pointed. "There's a church."

"Fire!" Flames licked at the base of some kind of structure in front of the church. That skirt. "Claire!"

Hillary sprinted, her eyes scanning the scene.

A priest and a bearded young man faced Claire. What were they yelling? They must be crazy. The young man looked straight at Hillary as she raced toward him. She cut past the shoulder-high vines and headed for the fire.

"Confess your sins," the young man shouted at Claire. "Now!"

"Stop!" Hillary shrieked, looking for water. There it was. A coiled hose, in front of the church.

Hillary shouted, "Claire! I'm coming!"

The priest yelled, "You will be forgiven!"

Claire screamed, "No, no, no!"

"Confess! You'll be forgiven!" shouted the young man.

"Confess to what?" Claire screamed.

The young man turned suddenly and was running to the spigot.

Close behind Hillary, Paisley sped toward the priest, pulling off her necklace as she ran.

Hillary yelled at Paisley, "Water, Mamma! Water!"

A blond man pivoted to cut Paisley off, but too late. She slipped by him and ran to the priest, stretching out her necklace at arm's length.

Hillary reached her wild-eyed daughter just as Claire looked down at her skirt. Hillary caught the glint of flames reflected in Claire's eyes before she slumped forward, limp and silent, her chest pressed into a rope binding her to a wooden post behind her.

52
HILLARY

Flinging away her tote and car key, Hillary stepped into the burning kindling, pressed her body full length against Claire's and wrapped her arms around her.

Hillary leaned down to run her hand over Claire's skirt, feeling for heat.

Hillary stamped on the flames dancing at their feet and screamed. "Water! Water!"

She leaned back and pulled on a rope binding Claire to the post.

"Water! Get water!" She reached around Claire, feeling along the rope for a knot.

It wasn't rope. It was a thick bungee cord.

Hillary stomped, smothering flames as she embraced Claire, her fingers finding the bungee hooks. She shoved the hooks against each other but there was no give. "A knife! A knife! Water!"

She twisted her head and spotted the hose. Why

wasn't the bearded man turning the water on? "Mamma!" Hillary screamed. "Get the hose!"

Behind the priest, Paisley threw her strangling cord over his head. She stretched out the ends, choking him, and yelled, "Get the water on!"

The priest fell to his knees and tore the necklace away from his throat. "The hose—Xavier!" he yelled.

Hillary turned to see the bearded young man at the front of the church. Hope flared, but he took precious seconds twisting the spigot before water gushed out.

"Hurry!" she screamed, stomping the flames beneath her feet.

The young man hauled the thick hose toward the fire. As the hose uncoiled, it cracked. A geyser of water shot high into the air. Wasted, thought Hillary. Too far away to reach the fire.

"Get in here!" Hillary screamed. "Get this fire out!" Her feet were feeling warm.

The blond man was throwing wood slats into the fire, grunting like a pig rooting out under the oaks.

Paisley ran behind the blond man and threw her cord over his head. She pulled. He fell to the ground gasping. She tugged harder and he fell silent.

The priest grabbed at his throat. "Xavier, stamp…" He coughed. "… it out." The priest collapsed, his face planted in the dust.

Hillary's feet danced as the fire licked her Adonis sneakers. Claire had on her Nikes, and Hillary flashed on a hope her daughter's shoes would be some protection from the growing flames.

"Help!" she screamed. Hanging on to the post with one arm, she yanked up her culottes, stuck the silk fabric into her waistband, and kicked the burning kindling away from the base of the post. "Get in here!" she yelled. "Get this fire out!"

The bearded man jumped in, his sneakers crushing the burning leaves and slats of wood.

Paisley ran to join them and pounded her shoes on the embers. Stamping in a crazed tarantella, the three of them circled around Claire, angled out away from the post, stock-still and motionless.

53
HILLARY

His tattoo glistening in the heat, Xavier shoved the bungee hooks against each other, twisted them and pulled them apart. As he flung the length of the bungee to the ground, Claire's shoulders slumped against his chest. He reached down and loosened the bungee at her waist. As she sagged forward, he turned her, lifted her, and cradled her in his arms. He ran up the church steps, her legs dangling along his side.

"Give me my daughter!" Hillary screamed. She ran after Xavier. He strode toward the open doorway into the church. As she ran alongside them, Hillary checked Claire's legs. Her calves were blistered. The singed edges of her rainbow skirt rubbed against her thighs. Her Nikes encased her feet. Hillary prayed the thick, cushioned soles had kept the heat to a minimum.

Inside the church, Hillary shouted for him to give

Claire to her. Needles of sunlight stabbed through holes in the roof and lit up Claire's blisters. Hillary could see that none were broken open. She had to get Claire's shoes off. Or was it better to leave them on? Her own feet were warm but not all that hot.

Xavier turned and laid Claire in Hillary's arms, tears in his eyes. "Take her to the altar. I'm getting something to bring her awake." He ran off toward a door at the far end of the sanctuary.

Hillary cradled Claire and bent to her daughter's face. After a second, she could feel breath on her cheek. Hillary sagged with relief and carried Claire past a crumbling fresco. At the sight of three women painted onto the sanctuary wall, bundled together and standing in flames, Hillary's heart skipped a beat.

As she rushed toward the altar, Hillary stumbled, cried out, and Claire fell onto the stone-cold floor. Xavier ran back, scooped up Claire and carried her toward the door. "I'll take her down." Hillary's heart raced. They had to doctor Claire. What would help? Her water bottle. Her tote! Still out in the dirt. Her phone!

"Got your phone?" she asked Paisley, now running beside her.

Paisley pulled her phone out of her bra. "No service."

It seemed to take hours, but Hillary neared the door. Xavier held the limp Claire and nodded at oil lamps on a little table by the door. "Light one for each of you. It's dark on the way down."

54
FATHER TOMMASO

Tommaso spit dirt from his mouth. He groaned. What happened? He raised his head a few inches until the pain in his neck stopped him. He lowered his face back to the ground. His nose hurt like hell. He turned his head to the side. He lay still, blinking against the sunlight.

Was that a body in the dirt nearby? Tommaso pushed his hand against the ground and raised himself so he could see. Oh, no. It was Albert, not moving a muscle. What happened?

That woman. That garrote. "Albert," he croaked. "Albert." The man lay inert. "Albert, wake up!"

Nothing.

Tommaso collapsed onto the dirt. He lay panting and sweating. Albert. Where were the others? He blacked out.

55
SISTER FREDERICKA

Fredericka stared at Vito. "You don't have to watch me every second, you know. I was called to be here."

Vito shook his head and sighed. "You are a brave woman, courageous as a man." He finished returning the place to what it was before Tommaso's attempt to drive the demon from Claire.

Just then they heard the heavy church door slam shut. And the sound of feet pounding against the stairs.

Xavier burst into the open lighted space, carrying Claire in his arms. "Help. Vito! Get water into the Boxio. We've got to run cool water over her legs." Claire's eyelids fluttered, and she began to moan. He set Claire on the lounge.

Hillary placed her daughter's legs so they were over the sink. Vito handed her a cup of water and she drizzled it over Claire's calves. "We've got you. You're safe."

Fredericka said, "Thank you, Xavier." He stood nearby, watching Claire be taken care of.

"How could you do this to her?" Hillary hissed at Xavier. "Who was that priest and that blond guy?"

Just then, Albert staggered into the open lighted space, dragging Father Tommaso at his side. Albert collapsed on the ground next to the shelf holding his tat supplies, yelling for help.

Claire screamed, "Get...away!"

Fredericka watched Vito shepherd the barely conscious priest into the altar room.

"That's Albert on the floor." Fredericka nodded in his direction. "And it's Father Tommas—" A sharp jolt under her feet interrupted Fredericka.

The LED lights dimmed and flickered.

Dirt particles fell from the ceiling.

A clay tile above the wrought iron shelf tumbled off the wall. The corner of the tile hit Albert in the temple and broke in two as it hit the ground. Albert lay motionless and silent.

From the other room, Vito cried out, "The cross fell off the altar."

Thunderous booms crashed against the door at the top of the stairs.

56
HILLARY

For a few minutes, no one moved. Nothing else fell.

Hillary ran through the tunnel, up the stairs and pushed against the wrought iron door. The door wouldn't give. She rammed into it with her shoulder, hard. Not even a fraction of an inch. The earthquake must have shaken the church's ceiling to the ground. They were trapped in the catacomb. She prayed Ed was on the way.

Hillary tended to Claire with Fredericka's help. They took Claire's Nikes off. The shoes had insulated her feet from the flames. Her legs were blistered but none had broken open. The cool water helped, and Claire rested. Hillary asked if Fredericka was all right. "They never hurt me. The Holy Spirit was with me. I think they were afraid of me."

Hillary nodded, grateful the plucky nun had been down in the catacomb with Claire.

Albert lay motionless on the floor next to the shelf. Frederika went to him and felt his carotid for a pulse. She made the sign of the cross over him, pulled a white silk scarf from around her shoulders, and placed it over his face. She looked at Hillary. "God rest his soul."

Hillary went back to the altar room for some water to drink. Vito was murmuring to Tommaso, bent over in a folding chair. "Albert is dead," she said. Vito shook his head. The priest gave an agonized cry.

"We need water to drink," Hillary said. Vito poured from the big plastic bottle, and Hillary took a cup for Claire to drink.

Hillary could hear shouting. She ran through the tunnel, up the stairs and pushed against the wrought iron door again. It wouldn't move. She put her ear to the metal.

There came a long, low whistle. It must be Ed. He and Jean must have arrived. A faint voice called, "Genevieve!"

It was Ed. She screamed and pounded on the door. "Call an ambulance! Claire is burnt!"

She heard sounds of scraping and crashing. He must be digging his way through rubble.

She pounded and screamed, "We're behind this door! Can you hear me?"

Nothing.

She ran back down to the open lighted place. Claire was silent and wide-eyed, looking at her legs, lying across the top of the Boxio sink. Hillary took

Claire's hand. "Your father is outside. He can't get in yet. The ceiling must have fallen and is piled up against the door. We can't get out of here. Yet."

Claire closed her eyes. Hillary looked at Fredericka, who nodded. Hillary continued, "I know he's called for help. You are going to be alright."

SUDDENLY THERE WAS ED, STRIDING INTO THE ROOM, bending to kiss Claire on the forehead and yelling, "Sofia and Mario are sending help." Jean was behind him, giving the place and the people a hard-eyed assessment.

Hillary jumped up and pointed at Claire.

Ed knelt next to Claire and patted her hands.

"I've got your tote," he said to Hillary, and put it on the long table. He frowned at the sight of the man on the floor with his face covered with a white scarf.

Hillary grabbed her tote and pulled out her water bottle. She opened it and directed a trickle of fresh water back and forth over Claire's blistered legs.

Ed shook his head. "There is a thick layer of rubble all over the church floor. Help is on the way …."

Jean looked in the altar room. "Let's get back and clear more rubble." Ed nodded, kissed Hillary and Claire, and followed Jean down the tunnel.

57
HILLARY

Hillary went into the altar room. Vito was bent over beside the priest, rubbing his back.

"Can you come into the other room?" Hillary said. "I need your help."

The priest shook his shoulders and moaned softly. Vito frowned.

"I need help reading some papers. In Italian."

The priest rocked back and forth. Vito put his hand under Tommaso's elbow. After long seconds, the priest bent forward. Inch by inch, he straightened to a near standing position. He steadied himself against Vito's arm. "We have failed," he muttered. "God help us now."

Hillary went and stood by the long table. Claire was resting on the lounge, Fredericka beside her in a folding chair.

"We are trapped, but help is on the way," Hillary

said. "Have a seat, everyone. I have something Mother Catherine's auntie sent along." Fredericka nodded, a half-smile on her lips.

Vito helped Father Tommaso lower himself to the camp chair. Paisley sat at the long table, doodling on a piece of paper. Xavier sat on the rug; next to the lounge, his arms encircling his bent knees, his head bowed.

Hillary pulled Aunt Eleanora's flat purse out of her tote. She took one of the papers from the purse and studied it for a minute.

She stretched out the paper in Vito's direction. "Can you translate this into English?"

Vito took the paper and scanned the page. He nodded somberly at Hillary.

"Please read it out loud," she said.

Vito's smooth baritone filled the room as he spoke. "Certificato di Nascita. Abandonment Certificate and Related Record of Birth." A hush fell over the room.

"Record of Birth, born on 15 March 1993, in Voce Sotto, Province of Perugia, Region of Umbria, a male child of unknown parents, abandoned, to whom baptism was administered *by Father Joseph Paul Fortunato* and to whom was given the names *Xavier* Esposito *and the surname of* Innocenti, the godfather being *Lorenzo Bozzano, a servant* domiciled in *Voce Sotto*, and godmother *Eleanora Bozzano, a landlady* domiciled in *Voce Sotto.*"

Xavier sat up, slack jawed and wide eyed, silent, watching Claire's legs. The water in the tiny sink riffled and sloshed up. It ran down over the side and dampened the rug where Xavier was sitting.

"An aftershock," said Vito. A niche cover tile tumbled from the wall to the ground, a foot away from Tommaso. He sat up quickly.

Hillary lifted the other paper from Aunt Eleanora's purse and scanned the lined page of handwriting. She handed it to Fredericka who looked it over and gave it to Tommaso.

"This is for you, Father," she said. "Translate for us, per favore."

Tommaso sat up, took the paper and looked it over. His jaw dropped, and his eyebrows shot up. He held out his hand. "Help me," he said to Vito.

It took long seconds for him to get upright. He leaned against Vito, holding the paper out in front of him, his eyes squinted.

His hand trembled, the paper shaking as he read aloud. "I, an unmarried woman of eighteen years, faced with the loss of my own and my family's honor, left Voce Sotto to shelter in a convent in Rome and after the birth of my son brought him to Abbey of the Wild Vines to be baptized and cared for by Father Joseph.

In order to pay for his care, I served in the … orfanotrofio," Tommaso stumbled over the word before he translated it, "orphanage as a wet nurse for abandoned infants. On my child's second birthday, I left to enter the order of St. Carlotta."

Tommaso breathed fast. "It is signed …" he whispered, “Beatrice Catherine…Beatrice. beh-a-TREE-cheh… “

He shook his head. “Beatrice. Beatrice Catherine.”

Fredericka stood. She looked from Tommaso to Xavier. “Yes. Beatrice Catherine. She is known to you on the phone calls as Mother Catherine.”

Tommaso gasped. “Her! All this time.” He collapsed to the camp chair and looked at Xavier, who was staring at him. “Beatrice. She was not at fault. It was harvest time, the grapes were ready early. I lured her to the vineyard, in love with her, but she refused me and…”

He dropped to his knees and crawled to the feet of Xavier. “Your name means ‘bright abandoned innocent one.’ I am sorry for my sin with all my heart. Forgive me.”

58
HILLARY

The room was silent. Another clay niche cover wobbled, then tumbled from the wall to the ground, splitting into three parts.

Fredericka said, "Long ago, Catherine forgave you, Tommaso, and kept watch over you and your son, from a distance, sheltered in our Casa de Carlotta."

Tears ran freely down Tommaso's cheeks as he stared at Xavier, who stood up, a stupefied look on his face. He looked down at Tommaso and said, "I am remembering a woman, singing me a lullaby, *'Ninna nanna,' Who do I give this baby to? Lullaby, lullaby oh, I'll give him to his mom who sings him a lullaby. Who do I give this baby to? I'll give him to the witch who cradles him for a week'.*" Xavier shook his head. "I cannot forgive you, Tommaso. You are no longer Father Tommaso to me."

Tommaso fell prostrate, face down on the rug.

Xavier looked at Claire. He dipped his hand into the small sink and sprinkled cool water over her legs. She smiled at him. He whispered, "Forgive m—" just as the heavy door banged open with a loud slam against the wall.

"Polizia qui! Polizia qui!"

59
HILLARY

Sofia marched into the room, Mario close behind.

"Claire," shouted Hillary, pointing to her daughter. "She's burned! The priest, the kidnapper, he's in bad shape."

Sofia stood ramrod straight, not a wrinkle in her navy suit, her voice steely. "Ambulances are parked below, in Voce Sotto. CRI is here." She waved in the direction of four muscular volunteers. "They will carry them down the hillside."

Hillary pointed to Vito and Xavier. "They are kidnappers, too."

Sofia nodded to Mario, who cuffed the two unresisting men.

"Down the hillside with them, in the van and take them to the transit prison," said Sofia, as Mario led Xavier and Vito towards the tunnel.

"The worst fiend of all." Hillary pointed to Albert. "Albert. He's no threat anymore."

Sofia nodded. She waved over one of the CRI volunteers. "Carry this creature to an ambulance though it's too late, thank God," she said.

As the CRI volunteer walked to the wrought iron shelf, it began to wobble. Sofia held it upright and pressed against the wall as the volunteer hefted the dead weight of Albert onto his back and headed for the tunnel.

"Aftershocks," she said, looking around at Hillary, Ed, and Fredericka, "Andiamo. Let's get the hell out of here." She let the shelf crash to the earthen ground.

60
HILLARY

The fountain burbled its soothing rhythm. Hillary relaxed in the swing out on the Casa di Carlotta rooftop garden. Claire had been released from the hospital, her calves wrapped lightly in gauze, and she now lay stretched out on the patio recliner. Paisley sat next to Hillary, sketching on a pad.

Hillary tried to follow Ed's story of why it took them so long to get to Wild Vines. He said, "Jean's client Giulia was afraid to tell the police. She showed him some notes her brother Carlo had written before he was shot to death at that Marina March."

"Marina March?"

"That's what Sister Fredericka was in when she was kidnapped."

Hillary nodded.

"Giulia had seen her brother approached by some men rumored to be Mafiosi in the week before the march. She didn't think too much about it then, but after he was killed…"

"Ah," said Hillary. "Go on."

"Carlo's notes named Osteria Cantoro in Pisano as a secret meeting location. Giulia thought we should go there, question the owner, so we did, and it didn't take long for Pietro Cantoro to cave. He's a good guy mixed up with some bad dudes. He named Abbey of the Wild Vines as where they were taking the women."

"Didn't you see my text?" Paisley asked.

"Not 'til after we heard from Pietro. I called Sofia, and Jean, and I raced up to Wild Vines. We ran into the mess of the church ceiling all over the floor."

Hillary ran her fingers through her hair, twisted it into a knot and clipped it on top of her head. "Sister Fredericka's recovering in her room downstairs. Claire's here with us, thank God. It was Paisley and her necklace that saved us!"

Paisley drew out the necklace from her blouse. She whirled the ends in the air. Hillary applauded. "It was like being in some kind of Polynesian melodrama, so unbelievable, it was almost funny."

"Funny AF!" shouted Claire.

61
SISTER FREDERICKA

Fredericka wanted to be left alone. "Mother Catherine, I'm all right. Just exhausted and a bit bruised. Please. Stop hovering."

Mother Catherine wiped her forehead. "It's hot in this little room. I'm bringing you a fan." She was gone for five minutes, during which Fredericka fell asleep.

The cool breeze from the fan snapped her awake. She smiled at Mother Catherine. "Now the truth is revealed, and you don't have to hide your secret anymore."

"I don't know how you kept your wits about you." Catherine held out a plate of cinnamon-crusted snickerdoodles. "Your favorite."

Fredericka smiled. "The Holy Spirit places me where I'm needed. First helping out Mary and Delilah. Then taking on those misled men, supporting Claire and your Xavier, innocent in so many ways, led down a bad path for some time."

Mother Catherine said, "Horrible as it was, both the burning and the earthquake at the Abbey seemed to be God's way of revealing secrets."

Fredericka took a cookie. "God's work will go on. But the truth is not easy to hear. Xavier turned away from Tommaso and won't forgive him. I don't know how your son feels about you."

Mother Catherine nodded. "I've made arrangements to visit him this afternoon. Pauline will sit with you."

Pauline came into the room, carrying a page from her Bible project. "I can work on it at your desk. Today, I'm at 'this is my beloved son'."

"One of my favorites," said Fredericka. "Tell me how you will write it." She bit into her Snickerdoodle.

62
XAVIER

Xavier trembled in his cell. This afternoon, he would meet his mother, a day he never thought would come. He couldn't make himself take even a sip of coffee for fear he might throw it back up.

Anxiety boiled in his bowels, but his eyes longed to see her. He couldn't forgive his father, who was near death. Probably headed for hell. But maybe his mother could sit with him, talk to him, explain how it all happened. His mother, Catherine. Of all things, a nun.

He never met any nuns before Fredericka, barely knew any women at all. Only been close up to Trota and then the nun and Claire. He twisted his fingers. He stood and paced the stone floor, head bent.

What would he call her? Why did he agree to let her come? He gripped the bars. The cold metal smelled like a 50-cent euro. Why did she give him away? Was she even sorry?

A nun. Mother Catherine. Everyone's mother but mine.

"Guard!" he called. The guard walked to the cell. "Tell her I changed my mind. I don't want to see her."

The guard nodded and walked away. Xavier drew a deep breath and picked up the cup of coffee from his tray. He turned to the man in the cell next to his. "Is the coffee here any good, Vito?"

63
HILLARY

Claire said she felt well enough to go down with them to eat in the breakfast room. As they sat at the little table, Sister Fredericka joined them. "Xavier wouldn't see Catherine," she said.

Hillary nodded. "He hates her for abandoning him. But under it all, he loves her. I understand." She smiled at Paisley.

Paisley said, "Catherine gave him up because she was ashamed of what was not her fault. It was not him who was unlovable but the system that set up who's worth more and who's worth less. He'll have to pay the price of his crime, though.

Claire said, "He got tangled up with some bad dudes. But he's a good guy under it all. I'd love to go talk to him, Mom."

Hillary nodded. "I'll ask Sofia to arrange it."

• • •

In the old Carceri San Giuseppe visitors' room, Hillary could see Xavier on the other side of the bars at the small window. He looked pale and serious, and said nothing.

"Xavier, my mother abandoned me when I was ten years old," said Hillary. "I know that you suffered longer than that, but I'm here to tell you Mother Catherine looked out for you all these years. She baked special breads and treats for you at Easter and Christmas. Did you know?"

He shook his head. "Father Joseph said they were from my guardian angel."

"Catherine loves you," Hillary said. "She sent along Snickerdoodles today, but they won't let you have them until they've been inspected."

"It's too late now," he said. "I don't want anything from her."

"Let me tell you that holding a grudge against your mother is like you taking poison and thinking she will die."

He stared at Hillary. "You mean it will kill me and not her?"

Hillary pressed her palms together as if in prayer. "Forgiveness is a long journey. Only after years of struggle have I found the grace to begin to forgive. I hope you will take the first step soon."

He shook his head. "No."

She scooted over to make more room for Claire on the bench beside her.

Xavier's eyes lit up as Claire began to speak.

"Xavier, you are a beautiful young man. I've seen you in bad times and in good. When you have served time for your crime and are released, I feel sure you will find the right woman to love you."

Tears began flowing down his cheeks and wet his beard.

Claire said, "I will write to you when I get home to California. I feel like a sister to you, and I hope you will write back."

He reached his fingertips through the bars. She touched hers to his. "I will. You can be sure I will, Sister Claire."

64
HILLARY

Hillary asked Pauline to meet her in the chapel that evening.

"I want to thank you for your guidance, Sister," Hillary said. "I've been able to begin healing the estrangement from my mother."

Pauline smiled but said nothing.

Hillary went on. "I still feel guilty but over something else. At the university, I saw a painting of a Madonna. A Queer Alliance artist had painted the child in blonde curls with a pink gown and white bonnet. I blurted out that he painted baby Jesus as a girl, as if it was a bad thing." She shook her head.

Pauline let the quiet hold. After a few minutes, she said "It's how we've been raised. No version of the Bible with God's preferred pronouns will loosen the ancient grip soon. We're on a bumpy path up a hillside to plant new grapes. And we'll need new wineskins, as well."

65
FATHER TOMMASO

Tommaso lay in the hospital bed, wheezing and wondering. He had not recognized her. All those phone calls. Mother Catherine. Beatrice. Why hadn't he recognized her voice? He had loved her—beautiful and chaste young Beatrice. A perfect name. He never knew her middle name until now. Catherine.

His youthful passion had taken over, out in the vineyard. Why had she never told him what his crime had produced? Shame flooded his cheeks. Hot shame. She had known and kept watch over both of them all this time. He would be leaving an awful legacy. A father after all. A man like the Green man he loved.

He'd been sucked in by the Cardinal's Dei Patris scheme, a front for his Mafia family, holding in place the traditional family, sending them to kill Carlo, who knew too much. Tommaso didn't have time to try and prove what his gut told him was true. The Cardinal was getting away with murder, under the cover of holy church tradition.

Tommaso had no Vatican trial to worry about. Just the private humiliation of lying here dying from the damage he'd done to himself in his wild oats years before the Father called him to the priesthood. He waited too long for courage to tell the doctor of the symptoms he ignored so long ago.

My cause of death will not be made public. The Cardinal will come and go through the deathbed motions. The sanctity of the confessional. He is the master of keeping things secret, keeping it all in the family of the church. The traditions.

Father, forgive me. I didn't know what I was doing.

66
HILLARY

As she walked into the room, Hillary was drawn again to the huge window behind Jean's desk. He'd invited them to his office for a farewell celebration. There was the Vatican, a nation of power and tradition, the dome of its Basilica an immense hemisphere guarding the past. The sun was setting behind the buildings, making them appear larger than they were.

Jean stood next to her. "What kind of Father God demands that men love subservient women?"

Ed added, "What explains that kind of man?"

"Change. It's terrifying," Hillary said. "They are afraid."

"As my people would say," Jean replied, "they are a *Folie à plusieurs*—they infect each other with the madness of many."

Hillary shook her head. "Love means equality," said Ed, bending to kiss her.

Paisley pointed at the skyline. “We see a classic sunset over the Vatican. The end of the day. But, I have retitled my paintings as sunrises, time for new starts. And the judges agreed.” She looked at the others. “I just learned I won the Guggenheim.”

“Let’s drink to that!” Jean popped open a bottle of Champagne. He poured the bubbly wine. “I’ll miss you all!” he said, raising his flute in the air.

Claire laughed. “I’ll be back next year, to start university here.”

“I’ll stay on in Venice,” said Paisley. “I’ve been asked to teach at the retreat center.” She turned to Hillary. “Feel free to play in my cottage back home,” she said. “You’re welcome to my easel and paints.”

Hillary felt a giddiness come over her. Play. Paint. Make a mess. She reached to grab Paisley in a hug, just as Paisley turned away to flirt with Jean.

Hillary grinned at Ed. “That’s my mother,” Hillary said. “Full of adventure and fun.”

Claire laughed. “An F word, Mom.” She raised her new phone and backed away. “Let’s get a big happy family selfie!”

Hillary laughed, as Paisley joined in to pose for today’s picture. Tomorrow, they would fly home and meet tomorrow’s dangers. Working together, they could keep each other safe. Or at least pulled out of the fire.

THE END

ACKNOWLEDGMENTS

In the midst of backlash against equal rights and standing for women, I first acknowledge God, to whom I prayed almost every day asking if I was on the right track with this novel. God answered instantly every time—Yes. I thank my guides, editors and beta readers: Karen Freeman, Joey Garcia, Mike Henry, Alan Watt, Hallie Ephron, Melissa Walker, Isabella Maldonado, Rebecca Inch Partridge, Julie Davies; my fans especially my sister Jacki Burdick and friends Pat Minkle and Veronica Cupid; my patient and talented critique buddies Michele, Linda, Tarra, Danna; Bill, John, Pamela, Julie, Rose, Bonnie; Pam, Deborah, Gillian; my writing group Carolyn, Bruce, Mary, Aeisha, Seton, and Lori. What a blessing to have so many generous souls as my friends and advisors.

June Gillam, October 2024

ABOUT THE AUTHOR

June Gillam writes award-winning crime fiction exploring the shadow side of humanity, chasing her obsession to figure out what makes ordinary people mad enough to kill. Her books explore topics like women's empowerment, racism, greedy land development and intergenerational trauma. She blogs on these and similar topics at https://junegillam.medium.com A native of the Central Valley, June lives cradled between California's Coastal Range and the Sierra Nevada mountains. A co-founder of Gold Country Writers and San Joaquin Valley Writers, she also belongs to Capitol Crimes, Sacramento Chapter of Sisters in Crime; Northern California Publishers & Authors; and Town Square Writers.

June was honored in 2024 by the San Joaquin Valley Writers branch of the CA Writers Club with the establishment of the biannual June Gillam Award for Excellence in fiction, memoir or poetry. June loves it when her readers post Amazon reviews and follow her, and she invites everyone to visit www.junegillam.com and sign up for her monthly emails.

ALSO BY JUNE GILLAM

HILLARY BROOME CRIME NOVELS

Nest of White Crows

House of Hoops

House of Eire

House of Dads

House of Cuts

HILLARY BROOME CRIME NOVELS: Books 1-3, BOX SET

READING AND WRITING

Play Among the Stars: Find the Books for You

Writing in Small Groups the 4color Way

Creating Juicy Tales: Cooperative Inquiry into Writing Stories

Books Written By June Comarsh Gillam

CHILDREN'S PICTURE BOOK

Kiki's New Home

POETRY

Woman Song: For Better and for Worse

So Sweet Against Your Teeth: Poems from Childhood's Fall

The Raven's Nest by MUD, Published by Gorilla Girl Ink

June's Website www.junegillam.com

www.ingramcontent.com/pod-product-compliance
Lightning Source LLC
Chambersburg PA
CBHW011028190726
48290CB00011B/2752

* 9 7 8 1 7 3 2 4 6 4 2 9 2 *